WHO WERE
YOU WITH
LAST NIGHT?

by the same author

THE EARLSDON WAY

THE LIMITS OF LOVE

A WILD SURMISE

THE GRADUATE WIFE

THE TROUBLE WITH ENGLAND

LINDMANN

TWO FOR THE ROAD

ORCHESTRA AND BEGINNERS

LIKE MEN BETRAYED

WHO WERE YOU WITH LAST NIGHT?

Frederic Raphael

Jonathan Cape Thirty Bedford Square London

FIRST PUBLISHED 1971
© 1971 BY VOLATIC LIMITED

JONATHAN CAPE LTD
30 BEDFORD SQUARE, LONDON WC1

ISBN 0 224 00517 0

LINES FROM 'WHO WERE YOU
WITH LAST NIGHT?'
REPRODUCED BY PERMISSION
OF B. FELDMAN & CO. LTD

PRINTED AND BOUND IN GREAT BRITAIN
BY RICHARD CLAY (THE CHAUCER PRESS) LTD, BUNGAY, SUFFOLK

For BRIAN GLANVILLE

Who were you with last night?
Out in the pale moonlight?
Are you going to tell your missus
When you get home?
Who were you with last night?

'Tim Wicks.'

'Tim Wicks?'

'One of the chaps on the Development Board. Consultant. I'm sure I've mentioned him. One of Lambert Livingston's new brooms. Not one of the highups, but important in his way.'

'Influential?'

'Sorry?'

'I said influential?'

'Lambert Livingston's got a lot of time for him, put it that way. He's very thorough, is Tim. Used to be a quantity surveyor. Nothing much gets past him. Lambert Livingston's got a lot of faith in him.'

'Used to be a what?'

'Quantity surveyor. Look, Lo, why is it we always have to spend the first half-hour after I get home in different rooms?'

'If you'd sooner have a cold dinner, you've only got to say so. I get things as ready as I can, but I can't go beyond a

7

certain point until I hear the car. You like something hot when you get back, don't you?'

What I'd like to find is you stretched out naked on the hearthrug with a bit of something semi-transparent over your whatsit, or if not you then someone else, preferably someone else, a stranger about twenty-seven so I didn't have to think about her, so I didn't have to worry about who she was or what I was doing to her, someone with a pair of thick lips and hot eyes and Playboy tits and no one else in the house. That's what my idea of a hot dinner is, if you really want to know. That's my idea of something hot.

'Have you ever loved anybody, Hanson, really?'
'How do you know if you love someone? Not being able to do without them, is that what love is, or not wanting them to have a moment without you, is it that maybe? I don't know what it is. The happiest time I ever had was when I was in the merchant service, when we used to go to Amsterdam for instance and you could pick a woman like choosing a tie. I'm sorry but that was the life. Charlie Hanson, the nearest thing to Handsome! You didn't despise those women or anything, you didn't think anything about them like that. They had nice places, some of them, no messing, they're very clean and tidy, the Dutch, if you've ever been there, tile floors, electric fires or central heating, stoves some of them, nice lighting, you could make yourself at home so long as the tin lasted. Well, I'm not saying it's ideal. I'm not saying that I'd like to see my daughter being that to a bunch of sailors, I'm not saying that that's how the world ought to be, but I do know that that's when I was

8

happiest. Out with the boys, a few beers, some Bols, a few laughs, choose your billet and then back to the ship. We talked openly, we compared notes, what they did, what they'd let you do, which of 'em wanted extra. I've never told Lola about it. She knows I was a sailor, of course, and she knows what sailors are and all that business, but I've never mentioned the details. There's never been a suitable time. I don't know why.'

Sometimes, I sound like a monster saying this, only it's true, sometimes when I come back at night I drive along the lane and come to the house and I try to cheat the engine, I know she always recognizes the note and I try to cheat it, so as to be there and not there at the same time, I idle the engine or I gun it, as if I had lost my way for a moment and was going to be off again as soon as I got my bearings, anyway I look at the house (four and a half years of the mortgage paid, fifteen and a half to go – Christ, I shall be fifty-one, fifty-one, Jesus) and I wait for it to explode. I imagine it full of gas and she goes into the kitchen, strikes a match or that bloody battery-run affair, presses the button and whoomf, up she goes, the whole thing. There you are, I admit it, the whole lot of them – her, David, Annabelle, the lot – turning over and over in the sky like a lot of slow-motion pancakes. My wife, my children, the whole shebang. Well if I'm a monster then so're most people, if I'm any sort of judge. What astonishes me is how few people kill each other. Personally I've never so much as seen a dead person. We live in a century of unparalleled brutality and violence (I read the newspapers) and it's quite clear that there's a lot of it about, to put it mildly, because there are all these reports. I missed

9

the war by a whisker and then I was in the merchant service and that let me out of Kenya or Cyprus or any of those little shindigs so the result is I've never seen a dead person. I've seen ambulances with their lights flashing. I've seen people lying by the side of the road not looking too good with blankets over them and shattered glass like a shower of Glacier Mints all around them. I've seen crowds round people you couldn't see properly and that didn't look like they were coming up for the next round exactly, but I've never seen a dead person. I've been to funerals, my mother's for a start, but I was at sea when she died and they'd nailed her down by the time I came sprinting into the cemetery. They were already lowering away and I had to take their word for it she was inside. I wouldn't go to the hospital to see Annabelle or David born either. That's the woman's side of things, I don't see anything to be gained going. I don't mean I was indifferent; I care a lot about my kids. Maybe that's why I sometimes think of them dead. Maybe caring is more than I can stand really. Maybe people mainly want to kill what disturbs them. These blokes that go after little girls and that — I have kittens every time Annabelle goes out — maybe they're driven to kill them because they're so bloody vulnerable-looking. That may sound silly, but I mean something by it, something that I've experienced myself. You have a woman on the verge of tears, Lola sometimes, and you dread her crying and yet you hear yourself saying the very thing that'll push her over the edge and then, when it's too late, you could kill yourself. Well, if there isn't a parallel there I'm a Dutchman. (If I were I'd live in Amsterdam and that's a promise.) These men when they've shot their lot and strangled some poor little kid, they're so bloody pathetic,

10

aren't they? They're so empty, so — well, they certainly don't have goat's eyes and cloven hooves and that's for sure. It's the same thing; they care about the kids, that's the funny part, I'm sure of it, they care more about them than all the weeping mums and the angry dads. I'm not glossing it over, I'm not saying anything to excuse them because I don't excuse them, but they give those kids a kind of attention — it may sound funny — which the parents don't give them. They realize the point those kids have reached, they realize how they're on the verge of something terrible, horrible, something unlike anything they've been before, these little kids of nine and ten, on the verge of loneliness, wankers' ridge coming up, and they give them the whole of their lives in one quick bash. O.K., I'm sentimentalizing it, I'm making excuses in a way for them and they probably don't think any of the things I think they do. They probably just want a quick sniff of virgin knicker, maybe. But I can see more in it than that, I can see how they must care for those kids. I mean, while they're with them, those kids are their whole world, aren't they, and what moves them is how vulnerable they are, must be. I remember kids at school cried when you looked at them; you couldn't help looking at them. I didn't cry easily. In fact I hardly cried at all. You can tell by people's skins if they cry easily, people with the blood showing, they're the tearful ones, people who're tight in their skins, they've got the blood near the surface and they're the easiest to hurt. I wasn't strong but I was tough. If a man talks honestly about himself he'll always sound like a monster. (When you're asked by your kids to be a monster, you never find it very difficult do you? It's natural, that's what's so frightening.) And women, they like you to be a monster too sometimes, not in the house, but in bed, they like to think you're uncontrollable, you might kill them, they like that, like a bad dream you wake up from just in time. Lola never looks at me so admiringly as when I've had my hands round her throat. They like that, women. A chief stoker told me that trick on almost my first voyage, said his old woman liked him to choke her when he was having her, choke her till her eyes popped out of her head, only way he could be sure of her getting the big bang, that's what he told me. Chief stoker! Would be, wouldn't he? I wasn't strong, but I never showed I was hurt. No one ever saw me cry if I could help it. Hanson never blubs, I remember a big bloke saying when one of the kids was crying after he'd been kicked or something in a puntabout, up at King Edward's Hammersmith this was, when I was there, before my old man was moved up into Essex. No one ever made me cry because I didn't hang around waiting for it. Only I remember sometimes, I remember once and I can't even remember whether it was at school or during the holidays, during a holiday we spent down near Felixstowe it could have been, I remember standing in a field with the wind blowing and lots of yellow flowers, quite complicated flowers I remember so I couldn't believe they could be weeds they were so involved, such shades and very violent in the wind and the sun and I stood there—a little red cottage over to the right with a bicycle leaning against it and washing stretched in the wind—and I cried and cried. I remember the taste of the wind mixed with the tears and the snot, about eleven or twelve I guess I was, and I cried my heart out and I can't remember what about. My dad never belted me. He was away a lot and my mother was overworked—I suppose

12

most mothers are overworked, poor bitches – only she never said anything to hurt me. I wonder why I hated her so much. Why I still hate her even though I saw her put in the ground. I think I hate her because – this is only a rationalization of course – I hate her because she made the world seem so bloody huge, so bloody gigantic and I could never be more than something minute in it, something that could only attract attention if I did something wrong. The best thing that could happen, this was really what she thought, was that you never got noticed at all. The only people who got noticed were people who got summonsed, and that was something my mother dreaded more than anything, being summonsed. 'We won't be summonsed, will we?' I can hear her saying that now. She had a fantastic respect for the established order, policemen, the royal family, notices even, anything official, anything with BY ORDER on it, scared the life out of her, those things did. I don't know whether the old man was like that because I hardly have any memory of him. He never played with me much. I don't ever remember him laughing. Whether he liked it or not, I mean whether or not he subscribed to the same ideas, he was part of the official world. I think Mum saw him as a kind of notice-board, blank unless there were some instructions to be given. And she was always threatening me with him, even though he never did anything to me. 'I'll have to tell your father.' As if it was only bad news she ever told him, only bad news he ever wanted to hear. When I did something I was proud of I'd ask her sometimes was she going to tell Dad and she'd look at me like she wanted to say, 'Why should I, do you *want* me to?' As if I'd hurt her feelings. She was one of those broad, busy little women, always willing to do anything for me, but not much *with* me. I was an independent kid I suppose and it probably didn't occur to her I wanted anything from her. I hated her calling me more than anything else, the way she'd call my name, for dinner or whatever it was I mean, 'Char-leeeeeeee,' on a rising note thinner and thinner (music's never meant much to me), stand wherever she happened to be or come to the back door and shout out 'Charleeeee,' never mind what I was doing, on and on until I came. I never told her I didn't like it. I think she maybe thought I did, thought it was a token of love. I believe she did think that. Anyway she always cooked the things I liked, lots of fried stuff, kitchen full of smoke, she didn't mind, onions, anything she knew I liked she tried to do. I remember this windy day and the yellow flowers and I stood in that meadow and I cried and cried. Makes the tears come now thinking of myself and I don't have the faintest idea of what I was crying about. There were cars going down to the coast, I seem to remember, but at an odd angle, only just visible down below an iron fence, one of those bent iron fences you get round estates where they graze cattle (there's one not far from the Development Area, not far from West-fleet) streams of cars, Christ maybe it was before the war, maybe I was only five or six. Could it have been? I seem to remember cars unless that was another time and we had no car in those days, yes and the smell of cowpats. Had I stood in a cowpat? I wasn't afraid, I'm quite sure of that, I wasn't afraid of what would happen to me or anything like that and I hadn't hurt myself, but I do seem to remember those yellow flowers and dried cowpats in this field (no cows) and the taste of the wind and I cried and cried. I felt *cold*, even though the sun was shining, shining on those yellow flowers

14

till they looked — they looked like rancid butter, glossy, acid.

'I don't mind what I have. You don't have to go to a lot of trouble. I'd just as soon you didn't.'
'I know what you'd say if I dished up a cold dinner.'
'What would I say? Because I don't know what I'd say.'
'You'd say, "Some welcome".'
'I don't think I would. When have I ever said that?'
'When have I ever dished up a cold supper?'
'I don't think I've ever said "Some welcome" in my life. Not in that tone of voice.'
'And I hope you never do.'
'Then what makes you so certain that's what I'd say?'
'I can just hear you.'

I'm very fond of her sometimes. Fond, just that. If that doesn't sound like much, that's because people expect too much. For me feeling fond of Lola isn't nothing; it's quite a lot, it's almost enough, as a matter of fact. I sit in the chair with the evening paper over the arm and my head slightly sideways as if I weren't really reading, as if something had just accidentally caught my eye, something I *ought* to read, when I was in the middle of talking to her, and I catch myself thinking, 'I'm really quite fond of that woman.' She'll be coming in with a Pyrex dish and her face all shining with steam and I think I haven't done so badly and I don't know what I'd like then. I think I'd like her to shut up. I'd like her not to tell me about anything she's done or anything that's happened to David at school — but it never happens. David's nearly fourteen now. Fourteen. Big bush and all and

15

he's still a crybaby. He's got that skin with the blood near the surface and he's always either on the verge of tears or actually in tears. It's amazing. I get the same feeling with him I used to get with those kids at school. I want to belt him. I don't, except by accident, but sometimes I want to so much I have to sit on my hands. If I hadn't got a family I'd be quite a normal bloke I think sometimes. How the hell does it happen? As if I didn't know. I don't know, it really riles me, that kid sitting there with his eyes full of woe and his balls bursting with the stuff and him chucking away handkerchiefs stiff with it if I'm any judge. The number of new handkerchiefs that kid gets through! Always helping himself to mine. He keeps those people in business. And yet these are things I can never talk to him about, except in the most general, *serious* way. I have to give him love, advice, help, all that stuff. Christ, we should go to sea together. We ought to be mates at sea and he'd get more from me, if we were strangers I mean, than he does from the present set up.

'Aren't you ashamed of yourself? With a son and daughter? Aren't you ashamed of yourself?'

'What've they got to do with it?'

'They look up to you. Depend on you.'

'I don't keep them short of food or shelter. No, I don't feel ashamed. Why should I?'

'And your wife?'

'She hasn't done so badly. I don't have to spend every spare moment I have with her, do I? No, I'm not ashamed of myself, why should I be?'

'The things you've done to her?'

'I've done nothing to her.'

'You call this nothing?'

'What's it got to do with her? That's what I don't see.'

'You must need your head examining.'

'We all do. Don't you? Especially you. But what can any-one do about them, our heads? Nothing. Isn't that why we don't have anything done? Heads there's nothing you can do with.'

'And tails?'

'Sorry?'

'Nothing. I was making a joke. Rather a weak joke.'

'Tails we lose.'

'You can say that again.'

'I told you not to talk to each other.'

'Look, what do you want with us? What's the big idea?'

'What makes you think there's a girl?'

'What did you say? Charlie?'

'I didn't say anything. What did you think I said?'

'I didn't catch. That's why I asked.'

'Well I didn't say anything.'

'Anyway you had a good night.'

'A good night?'

'With this Tim Wicks.'

'I thought you meant sleep. With Tim Wicks, oh well, you know. Not bad. It wasn't exactly a night out. We had a lot of things to sort out so we sorted them out. In that sense, yes.'

'You didn't spend all the time at his office?'

'Until dinner. We went out to dinner.'

'Anywhere nice?'

'One of these steak houses, place where you get charcoal grills. Blokes in chefs' hats turning over slabs of meat and charging fancy prices. Decent-sized steaks, I'll say that, but pricey. Red leather seats, soft lighting, not a bad place.'

'Doesn't sound it. I hope you weren't paying.'

'Not likely. No, the Board paid. Fair enough. We were on business.'

'Just you and Tim Wicks. Just the two of you.'

'What do you mean? Yes of course. Well, most of the time. Until the coffee stage—'

'I thought as much. Pity to waste leather seats and soft lighting on just the two of you.'

'If you mean by that—all that happened was Lambert Livingston joined us. He'd been to a function he'd had to go to. So he joined us for coffee. He'd been to a cocktail party, one of the organizations that'd be coming out to the area. People I'd got in touch with, manufacture sliding doors, I think I told you about them—'

'Not that I remember.'

'I think I did. Anyway, they seem to have bitten and they asked Livingston to come and have a drink with them which must be a good sign. *Was* a good sign from what he told us afterwards. So there you are, that's one thing I seem to have brought off.'

'One thing! You could sell anybody anything. What was it that man called you when you were with Vent's? The smoothest thing since Vaseline?'

'A salesman's as good as his product. I wouldn't mind catching up with the bastard who said that, incidentally. He went off with three cartons of bulbs, the big showroom bulbs Vent's used to sell. Never heard of again.'

'Oh well they could afford it.'

'Maybe they could; I couldn't. Stopped it out of my commission.'

'They never.'

'You ask them. They damned well did. Not that I blame them. After all, think how easy it'd be to make off with a crafty case now and again and say a customer'd nicked them. You can't blame them.'

'I'm glad you left them all the same.'

'Well when a job like this comes along. No, I shall sort that bloke out if I come across him again. Smoothest thing since Vaseline, I'd forgotten that. I don't know what's smoother than Vaseline, but he was it. These sliding door people, Crumps, they'd be mad not to move. If ever decentralization made sense, it makes sense for them. They're stuck in the inner suburbs, terrible access problems, and they can clean up on the property market if they get out. I told their managing director the lorry park alone'd fetch a quarter of a million. That's a bit of an exaggeration, but then that's property for you: today's exaggeration is tomorrow's price – if you're lucky. So anyway ... '

'You don't want me any more do you?'

'Don't want you? Whatever gave you that idea?'

'And afterwards?'

'Sorry?'

'After the coffee stage?'

'We went to a pub. Unexpected really. I never expected a man like Lambert Livingston to want to go to a pub, but he did. He wanted to talk informally and there was this waiter kept hovering over us with the Grand Marnier, I can think of worse things to be hovered over with but Lambert got irritated with him, quite understandably—'

'Lambert!'

'I told you—'

'You call him Lambert now?'

'We had a few drinks. If these people, Crumps, if they come out to Westfleet that's a big thing for me. Once the drift starts, the word gets around. You've got a queue before you know what's happened. So we went to this pub where they had a few acts, song and dance, that kind of business. Funny really, right in the middle of the new town this was, but a quiet street, houses, cars outside, and then this pub, packed out, right there in the middle of all these empty streets and these acts being performed. Amazing.'

'Sounds like quite an evening.'

'Then I'm describing it badly. It was just a business evening. I couldn't watch the show much because I was trying to listen to Lambert, hear what he was saying.'

'Well at least you do your business in interesting places.'

'Think I wouldn't sooner be at home? How's it going in there? I'm starving.'

'What time do the pubs close?'

'Pubs? What do you mean?'

'What time do the pubs close? What do you think I mean?'

'Where? Westfleet?'

'Where else?'

'I don't know. Eleven. Half past. I don't know exactly.'

'Then why didn't you come home when the show was over? If it was only half past eleven? If you're so keen on being at home?'

The thing about murder, if what I've read is correct, is that it's usually a spur-of-the-moment crime. It's not thought about. Most of the murders you read about, except those of casual strangers by people who remain unidentified, are the failures. After all, if the financial news was only bankruptcies, not many people would be tempted into business. Successful murders are never recognized, like successful spies. I have never in any way advertised my dislike, or hatred if you prefer it, of my wife. I've been extremely reticent. I haven't complained to people at work. I assume the neighbours think we're devoted. I haven't even mentioned any possibility of disagreement to my solicitor. We had a solicitor when we bought the house. I wanted to have it in our joint names. He felt obliged to point out that such an arrangement could be awkward if there was a marital dispute. If there was a possible divorce, half of the house might belong to Lola. I thanked him for telling me the facts but said that the possibility to which he referred was not one I cared to entertain. I can be very grammatical if roused. The truth is, you can't go through life expecting the worst. Nevertheless, of course, one does — well, not expecting, but hoping. I'm not worried about Lola having half the house in case of a dispute because to my mind there's always been a dispute, and there's only one way it can end and that's by her being eliminated. I'm not tearing any house of mine along the dotted line. Now the odd thing is that I have no desire actually to kill her. I mean I don't fancy throttling her or sticking a knife into her. Thoughts like that actually appal me. That's why the first intimation that I ever had that I wanted her out of the way was so, well, impersonal, just this picture of the house full of gas and whoomf, I was a free man. Free? I have no wish to be free in order to do anything else. That will be the great strength of my position subsequently. I have no mistress, no secret life; I'm one of the dullest men you could hope to know. There's nothing to come out, nothing. My secret life, such as it is, consists of a possible trip to Amsterdam for instance, or a week on a beach in southern Spain where I understand adventure comes quite cheap (years ago a shipmate told me you could get a woman for 1s. 9d. in Barcelona, though, of course, that was when the pound was stronger), and these little fancies of mine are locked so tight in my mind that when I think of going to Lola's funeral – and of course the kids would have to be spirited away somehow too – I never have any plans for the afternoon. I should be too miserable for a start. Of course I would. I think I should make a very convincing widower because I would undoubtedly be genuinely upset.

'Get dressed.'

Something awful happened to Lo's knockers after Annabelle. Maybe she fed her too long or too much or didn't wear the right kind of brassière. Anyway they went long and droopy. I couldn't fancy them any more, but that doesn't mean that I didn't once upon a time find Lo as attractive as anyone. The funny thing was, I could never fancy her and care for her at the same time. That's probably the result of what happened before we were married. But I do care for her; I've always tried to give her what she wanted and I don't think I've treated her badly. What possible reason could I have for killing her? We've got no history and it's not, as I say, as if I had anywhere else to go. I haven't got a better life to go to. She's not keeping me from anything I'd rather have, not on the face of it. She doesn't own a thing, except half my house, which I can hardly be accused of scheming to get hold of. I'm completely in the clear. Why do I dream of having her out of the way then? Why don't I just leave her? Well, you could ask that question of a million men in these islands and elsewhere and what would they say? I don't know. Well, I do know in a way. She'd still be around. I'd feel guilty. I'd feel her pointing at me all the time, like Lord Kitchener. And more than that, I'd miss her; I'd want to go back to her. Two days on your own and you'd go back to gaol, wouldn't you? They do. I shouldn't be able to stick it out. I should only be able to stand it if I knew that she wasn't there to go back to; I shall have to kill her in order to stop myself from running back to her. So why should anyone ever suspect that I'd wanted to do away with her?

'Don't. Go away.'
'I'll give the orders.'

The question arises, of course, how to do the job. That's what's held me up in part, but not as much as you might think. You can get rid of people, after all. For a start, there are people who get rid of people for you. I've seen films about them and I've read articles about them. They don't come as cheap as nooky in Barcelona, but there are cities where a few quid'll get rid of a bloke you don't like. I wonder if anyone would pay anyone a few quid to get rid of me. I don't reckon I make many enemies. I'm not an aggressive type and being a salesman for a product I believe in, this Westfleet Development Area, I try to do a decent job, I don't trick people, I don't fail to deliver. I reckon I'm as trustworthy as anyone needs to be. I don't think I'd get the old stiletto in the back that quickly, honestly, but it makes you wonder what it'd be like living in a city where a few quid'll get rid of a bloke. It must be quite a temptation if you've got a few bob and anyone that crosses you you can have done away with. Anyway, that's Baghdad or some-where, you couldn't import one of those chaps without having to do a lot of explaining, especially now they've tightened up on immigration, which I'm in favour of. Never mind, there are people'd take care of it for you in this country, there must be. The underworld's always fascinated me. It goes back to my mother I think. The underworld terrified her, like summonses. We lived between the law up above and the dark forces down below. She was an Edgar Wallace addict; he terrified the daylights out of her. All those blokes who wrote about secret powers, hidden forces, they got to her as well. Gregory Sallust. Now the funny thing about the underworld is that in spite of her believing in it absolutely, in spite of her thinking that we lived in constant peril, she never lost so much as a sixpence in all her life so far as I remember and never had anything remotely peculiar happen to her. She might have been living in the Garden of Eden the amount of trouble she had in her life, but she was scared the whole time. Of course there were problems, but that's not what I'm talking about. She was afraid of forces, forces which, if they really existed, weren't remotely interested in her. Now I can see how ridiculous her fears were, how pathetic, and yet I sometimes think that I'm no better. What neither of us could bear to accept was

24

how totally unimportant we really are. I once met a man who had an uncle who believed that all sporting results were fixed. Every single one. Even the reserve games, the amateur reserve games. The way this bloke told it, he even managed to believe park games were fixed, he believed every single sporting result without exception in the whole country was bent. Now how could anyone come to believe a thing like that? But then how can anyone believe that everything you do is known to God? The fact is, it comforts people to think that, it makes them feel less insignificant. What they can't bring themselves to face are the great gaps in the universe. I was reading this paperback and more of us is holes than solid. More of the world is empty space than anything else. Somehow this made me think about killing Lo and afterwards. It isn't necessary to have anywhere to go, any definite destination. Freedom is existing in limbo. You don't have to have a purpose, in fact you're much better not. The whole world is full of emptiness, the universe is more nothing than anything else, the way this bloke told it. Well why not be the same way – happy being nothing? I used to feel bad at school because one of the boys once told me that you're always thinking something, you've always got some thought going on in your head, like on a pin-table with a perpetual ball, always bumping something into life, but I didn't have that experience. There were times when I didn't have a blind thought in my head, when I was absolutely without a thought in my head. This kid said it wasn't possible unless I was loopy. Now isn't it funny how willing you are to believe a thing like that? I went around afterwards for a long time trying to think what I was thinking, like trying to jump on my shadow. But there's no reason why you should think at all. Personally I'm trying to train myself to think as little as possible. What better way can there be of not showing guilt? When Lo is being buried there'll be no problem; I shall naturally feel terrible, with everyone watching me, upset, I mean, genuinely, that bit doesn't worry me in the slightest, I shall manage that like cream. But what about the long bit before and the weeks afterwards, how shall I get through them if my head's full of thoughts, if I keep going over things? My view is, no one will ever suspect you of murder if you go on looking as miserable afterwards as you did before. You can get away with anything so long as you're not too cheerful about it. Think of Crippen; no one rumbled him until he started enjoying himself with that bird he had on the side. Of all the things that society can imagine you wanting to kill your wife for, *nothing* is the one thing that will never occur to them. You can't think of nothing, can you? So you can't want it, if you can't think of it. Only it so happens that a long spell of nothing is exactly what I'm looking forward to; hence I have the one motive no one can ever detect and no cross-examination can ever expose. I'm going to go into a nice quiet coma, a period of meditative mourning. I shall be a rather pitiful object about the place. I shall have a glazed look in my eye. And then, when a decent interval has elapsed, people will begin to be anxious about me, they'll start trying to woo me back to the land of the living, because they'll be uncomfortable at me being so inconsolable, and only then will I slowly, reluctantly, in response to overwhelming public demand, fire my retrorocket and re-enter the earth's atmosphere. Only then, very slowly, will I start, as they say, to remake my life. And everyone will congratulate themselves on having coaxed

26

me into a smile and it will never occur to them to doubt that it was thanks to them that I've been persuaded to take a week off in, for example, the south of Spain. I'm absolutely determined not to be in a hurry to do anything. Equally, of course, I don't intend to set any timetable for killing Lola. I'm not in a hurry either way. Nurses, policemen and successful murderers have one thing in common: you never see them run. What's the hurry after all? She doesn't drive me mad or anything; she hasn't got a fortune I have to inherit by the first of the year; the very fact that I'm constantly planning her murder actually makes me quite devoted to her. It's only things you're afraid to admit to yourself that really drive you crazy. And Lola, in the nature of things, is very rarely out of my thoughts. I admit I do sometimes wish she'd do certain things differently. For a start, I wish she'd talk less. I wish she was more of a machine; I could have a lot of time for an intelligent robot, whereas she never seems to notice when I've had enough. On the other hand, that's no call to kill somebody, thump them yes, but not kill them. If I feel violent, that's another thing entirely. This murder has got nothing to do with hurting her. The actual killing, as I say, is just a mechanical necessity; it's nothing to look forward to. I'm not perverted after all. The killing is by the way. It's the time before and the time after, those are the areas which need thinking about: method and alibi. I've considered it, but on balance I'm not very keen on hiring people to do the job. My experience is that if you want something done properly you've got to do it yourself. I've become very good about the house for exactly that reason. I don't trust people today, I'm quite serious about that. And hire someone for a job like the one I'm talking about and he's never paid off, is he? However you try to conceal who you are and why you want it done and where the money's coming from, who wants to knock off a woman in a sub-urban house except her husband? But then of course if she's found dead at all the same thing applies. Suspicion can only fall on her nearest and so-called dearest. (Doesn't that say something about all this loving business? If people really believed husbands and wives loved each other, why would they always suspect a man of killing his wife and vice versa first thing? Unless killing the other person is the last stage of love, which is a thought.)

'Maybe I'm going to do something to you.'

When I have to stay overnight I go to bed in the Plan-tagenet Hotel at Westfleet at eleven o'clock, collect my key, go to my room and the next thing anyone knows about me is when they knock me up for breakfast. That means eight clear hours. I could be out the window into the car and over to Brands Manor by half past two, into the house, do the job and back again in time for an early call, say if I've got a working breakfast. I've often considered that, only you don't have to be too bright to see the flaws. It's fair enough in principle, but fatal in fact because after all they could almost certainly rustle up a witness who'd heard the car start up or who'd seen you outside the house or parked up the road or wherever you'd put it. Short of nipping over on a broomstick, the thing's either impossible or silly. Too many imponderables. And even if I managed without being seen, without leaving any obvious visiting cards, who else could have done her in but me? They'd find the cracks in the alibi because cracks there would inevitably be. So, there has to be a way of getting rid of her while I'm genuinely and honestly asleep in my bed in another part of the world. They might still try to crack me, but they wouldn't be able to because I would be honestly innocent and they could cross-examine me till their tongues knotted, they wouldn't get anything out of me because there would be nothing to get. Apart from anything else, that's an ideal situation, to force the investigation to centre on, to stand or fall on, an element which looks like your weak spot but in fact is the strongest in your defences. If you can get the enemy to strike where you seem weakest but are actually strongest they must fail. So she's got to die in a way that seems to need the presence of a third party when that third party *can't* be me. It has to be either a mystery or a tragedy. I read about a part of the country, a small town, which turned out to be built over some old disused mines and people used to disappear from time to time, the ground would literally open up and they'd disappear. I thought about looking for a job thereabouts, then having to move to be near the work, buying a house and then have Lo disappear one day, into the underworld so to speak. What you would do in that instance would be to ask the neighbours how dangerous the situation really was. Now it stands to reason they'd underplay it, because other-wise property values are zero, so you'd keep on saying how worried you were until they'd start to shut you up, because who wants to hear someone beefing all the time. Right, when the time comes and what you've often feared would happen actually happens, what's the result? They all feel so guilty they can't forgive themselves. NEIGHBOURS LAUGHED AT HUSBAND'S FOREBODINGS. Unless someone actually saw you tipping her down the chute, no one would ever think in a million years that you weren't a martyr to their indifference. A TOWN'S SHAME, you might even get a headline like that to carry round with you. I seriously considered that place, but the trouble there was, though it sounded a very dangerous locality, after all, you could never be sure when you might not disappear yourself. The best thing is undoubtedly to rely on what you might call assisted chance. For instance, in the case of the hole in the ground, it might have worked if one could have had a private hole no one else knew about, and then encouraged her to take walks in that direction. It might take a year, even more, but eventually one would be a tragic figure. Sooner or later she'd pitch in. And, in the meanwhile, one could live in hope, one would have something to live for, like having money on a horse every day without it costing you anything. If you lose you lose, but if you win, it's the jackpot. By this stage, I suppose I must sound like a complete bloody maniac, you'll wonder how I manage to hide my horns and my hairy tail. Well, I still say what I said before, there are more people like me than not. I'm a freak only in that I'm honest with myself. If I wanted to balance the picture I'd point to the large bunch of flowers on top of the goggle. I'm an affectionate man. I'm also quite a generous one. I like to make Lo happy; I like to see her smile. I don't plan to kill her because I think she's a monster or anything like that. When I kiss her I don't sink my fangs into her; I enjoy it and I hope she does. I regret her knockers, as I say, but these things happen. I don't blame her. Only sometimes in bed she murmurs, 'Nipples, nipples,' and then I do feel a bit queer, I must admit, the way she says that, wanting me to

30

do her nipples, that upsets me occasionally, but it's part of life, you have to be a prude not to do a woman the way she wants. In fact sometimes it irks me she doesn't have anything she does want doing, doesn't seem to care what happens, that's when I get this violence thing, but it's the opposite of murderous; I want to poke her into life, not be left with a stiff. I don't care as long as she wants something, and something she wouldn't admit she wanted normally is best of all, that's when I feel as if the whole of ordinary life has blown away, all the fake has blown away, when she wants something she'd never talk about, something she'd never admit, when what she's so careful to be all the time, clean, neat, tidy, all those things, all mean absolutely nothing and I think yes that's it, that's bloody what it's all about, blind nothing, fighting with a stranger in the dark. If only she'd shut up. Only that's where we come back to this domestic thing. How many times, when you're hard at it, does a woman wonder whether she left the gas on or whether she stoked the bloody Aga?

'I wish you'd tell us what you want.'

The best thing would undoubtedly be some mechanical failure which would leave me not only beyond suspicion but the recipient of considerable sympathy. Suppose that one could time the house to fall down or burst into flames eighteen months from now. Suppose that one rewired it so that a short took place exactly so many hours from now. And it happened to be a day when one was in Neasden seeing some people. If the time between the work being done and the accident was great enough, how could anyone ever accuse one of having arranged it? It would be ridiculous. I could've used the same switch myself a thousand times. I could have rigged it up especially for myself. I could have *forbidden* her to use it. Think how tragic that would be. I could be known to have forbidden her to use it. The one thing they could never make anyone believe, the one thing they'd never believe themselves, would be the one thing that was true, that you'd arranged a fuse that didn't reach the explosive (I'm speaking figuratively here, of course, there'd be no suspicious circumstances) for a very long time indeed. Here's another idea; suppose Lola was on to me about central heating, as she has been, not that I blame her, we could do with a bit more warmth, and suppose I was worried, told a few people, well in advance, that I was worried that I might lose her unless I found a way of giving her what she wanted (I could ask Lambert Livingston for a big advance, which he'd almost certainly not give me) and suppose eventually I decided to do the job myself. I'm perfectly capable of that. Now wouldn't it be tragic if in giving her exactly what I wanted to give her, the thing that would make her happy, I happened to arrange the means of her destruction? It would be genuinely tragic. HUSBAND WILL NEVER FORGIVE HIMSELF. It would certainly be in the local and it might even be in the national press. I have no doubt that a number of women would want to comfort me. I'd be almost inconsolable. And what, let's face it, is more seductive to a woman than someone who's almost inconsolable? The only thing one would have to be certain of would be that she was there when the balloon went up. Something very simple could take care of that. For instance, you could say at break-fast that there was a call that might come to the house and could she be sure to be in in case it did? Since there would be no call, there would be no way of knowing that one had ever said anything about it and you'd be pretty sure she'd be there when H-hour finally came. The short circuit would have to be built into the system in such a way that there was nothing positive needed doing between the building and the explosion. Certainly you couldn't afford to have a trigger or switch that needed setting. It's amazing what they can detect after a fire say, the things they can reassemble, so it'd have to be a human error, something no one could ever have been expected to notice. MILLION TO ONE CHANCE KILLS WIFE. That's exactly what I'm after, a million-to-one winner. How could one be sure that the blow-up would take place exactly on the day planned? How could one be sure that she would suffer fatal injuries? I should suffer agonies of remorse if she were badly hurt. I don't think I could bear it. Death isn't a form of injury, after all; it's a different thing entirely. To have injured her, perhaps per-manently, would be more than I could live with. I'd have to make absolutely certain she was killed.

'What exactly do you want me to do?'
'I don't know. I haven't thought about it. Nothing. Any-thing. It'd be up to you.'
'You'd leave it to my discretion, is that what you're saying?'
'Yes. If you like.'
'It's your decision. It's not my decision.'

Answer me a simple question: how many motor accidents are really accidents? I mean, here are so many thousand

33

people being knocked off annually and how many of them are really accidents? *All of them?* Can you really believe that? It's a load of rubbish, only nobody talks about it because they know it's impossible in most cases to begin to sort the clever ones from the fools, the ones that work it out and the ones who can't stop it happening. How can you prove that a bloke meant to crunch his wife? How can you *prove* it? How many cases are there when a bloke or a woman, I'm not putting them in the clear necessarily, women, not by any means, how many times is one or the other left absolutely unharmed by an accident, so called, which does for the other one? Unless there's what they call a history, they can never prove it. Look, these two-car families, do they all have two cars out of the kindness of the husband's heart? I can't see it myself. What could be easier than to make some minute adjustment to the wife's car and then sit back and wait for the divi? It's not nice to think about, but it's a damned sight more undetectable than poisoning, for instance, because you don't leave anything inside her, there's nothing to be analysed is there? You can speculate, but you can't be sure. All those people killed, it makes you think. Driving always seems a bit lucky to me, I mean you miss this or that by so little, don't you? Overtaking or just coming along a narrow road there's only a foot sometimes between you and death, sometimes less, so you've only got to add one more imponderable to the situation, one surprise ingredient, and bingo, likely as not the extra straw'll break the camel's back without the camel ever guessing what happened. I might save up to buy Lo a car, now I come to think about it. What a ghastly thing, after all, to buy your wife a car, to save up and buy her a car and then have her go and kill herself first time out. It'd probably make the national press, something like that.

'It's not like it was when we were first married, naturally.'

The first house we looked at in the district I thought it was underpriced. That was what attracted my attention in the first place because I'm quite up in these things, in the value of property, obviously enough since I got involved with the Westfleet Development Board, it's opened my eyes, and this place, four bedrooms, detached house 1937, well I reckoned it was a gift at the price they were asking, if there was nothing wrong with it. I thought there had to be. I said to Lo that we should get there early and have a sniff round before the agent arrived, so we did and it was even better than I expected, I thought somebody must've made a mistake. 'There must be something wrong with it, Charlie,' Lo said, and I said, 'That's typical of you! Why should there be?' at the same time naturally thinking exactly the same thing. She'd put on a hat, tribute to Brands Manor I suppose, starting as she meant to go on and all that business, and it irritated me, putting on a show to look at a house. I'd put my best suit on myself, as if the house was looking us over rather than the other way about. Then the agent turned up and he was a young bloke, winklepickers and scurf and this sharp look about him as if he suspected we'd been nicking the daffs before he arrived, patronizing little sod, I thought. He kept saying what a bargain the place was and under-priced and in the end I just said to him, 'I only want to ask you one question and that is, what's the matter with it?' And he said, 'Matter with it? Nothing.' 'Then why's it so cheap?' 'You must ask the owners,' he said. 'I can't ask the owners. I'm asking you.' 'I rather assumed you must – you don't follow the papers, I take it, because – ' 'There hasn't been a murder here has there?' 'Lo, you don't have to – ' 'No, Mrs Hanson, I'm glad to say it's nothing of that sort. No violence, no ghosts, nothing like that. Do Fred and Cynthia Cresswell mean anything to you?' 'Fred and Cynthia Cresswell?' 'This was their house.' 'As I've never heard of them – ' 'Or the Leicester Case?' 'Wasn't that something to do with secrets?' 'It was indeed.' 'And this was their house?' 'This was Fred and Cynthia Cresswell's house. In fact it *is* Fred and Cynthia Cresswell's house. This is where they lived.' 'Well, no wonder,' Lo said. I looked round, I couldn't see anything so off-putting. 'No wonder what?' 'No wonder people don't fancy living here.' 'They only lived here,' I said, 'didn't they?' 'That's quite right.' 'They didn't *do* anything here. I mean, they didn't spy here. They went *out* to spy. Nobody complained about what they did here, did they?' 'As far as I understand very much the opposite. They seem to have been very decent people. The neighbours haven't been able to have a holiday since they left, because they always used to look after their cats. They can't say enough for them, as a matter of fact.' 'So,' I said, 'there's no question of our moving into an atmosphere of malice and suspicion.' 'Only if you don't like cats, I'd say.' 'Well, I don't think a thing like that – do you, Lo?' She wasn't looking too convinced. 'They were traitors, weren't they? Traitors to their country.' 'I thought they turned out not to be English at all – ' 'They wanted to betray us, didn't they? They didn't care what happened to us.' 'I must say,' I said to this agent, because I felt closer to him quite honestly than to Lo, because we seemed to want the same thing, which was to close the sale, 'I must say I think you've been very straight with us.' 'We're not in business to deceive people.' You'd think I'd called him a crook. 'I think we ought to think about it,' Lo said, 'I really do.' 'Think by all means, Mrs Hanson, but don't think too long, that's my advice, because a property of this type doesn't stay long on the market these days.' 'I still don't see why it's so little money, if it's so easy to sell.' 'The truth is, these people want the money fast, and those who want money fast can't be too particular about the price. That's a basic law of economics, I'm afraid.' 'Why're they in such a hurry? I thought they'd been sent to prison for years and years? What's their hurry?' Lo obviously thought she was being very smart. It must've been the hat. 'Well, there's talk of an exchange in the air, if you really want to know, this is confidential actually, so I'd be glad—' 'Oh we won't tell anybody,' Lo said. And I thought, who've you got to tell, it was as if only this character and Lord Mountbatten knew about it and now us. 'And if that's the case, they'll be wanting to take their money with them.' 'You mean they'll be allowed to take our money with them?' 'It'll be their money if we buy the house, won't it?' I wanted to cut this short. 'But they were spies.' 'Well they did a job as well, I daresay. They paid for the house. It's all perfectly legal.' 'That doesn't make it right,' Lo said, 'they're spies and traitors, they sold their country.' 'They weren't English. I'm not saying it ought to be allowed, but they weren't doing anything immoral or anything.' 'Are you saying that you don't mind them taking your money out of the country and—?' 'It'll be their money if we get the house. Look, they're bound to take somebody's

37

money because I mean this house is going to be sold sooner or later and probably sooner, right?' 'I suppose so.' 'And it's a nice place, you have to admit that.' 'I'm not saying it isn't.' 'Well then? Look,' I said to the agent, 'we'll call you this afternoon.' 'Fair enough,' he said, 'fair enough.' Outside I said to her, 'You know it's a bargain.' And she said, 'I know, but I wouldn't be happy.' I worked on her for hours and in the end she agreed that morals didn't really come into it. Only by that time she'd decided she didn't really like the kitchen.

'On an average how many times do you have intercourse each week?'

'With my husband you mean?'

'Well, yes.'

'You mean ... '

'Yes.'

'I don't know. It depends, doesn't it? When do you count the week from? From Monday or Sunday? Because some people do it one way and some people do it another.'

Lo said she'd sooner stay where we were. I didn't press her; it has to be a joint decision, doesn't it? So we missed that house and bought the one we have now, half as much again it cost me, the same house. She *is* like my mother. Spying, treachery, to her it's something absolutely repugnant. Personally I'm rather the opposite. I shouldn't mind being a spy. I don't mean screwing all the girls or being licensed to kill or any of that business (though I shouldn't object) I mean spying in the quiet, patient sense. I shouldn't mind doing it as a sideline, like those people who sell flowers and lettuce outside the front gate at weekends, acting as a safe house or something along those lines, not if the money was right. My view is there's time for more than one thing in life. And I may be wrong, but what could give more spice to one's life than getting away with something? It's not simply that it's worthwhile in itself, for the money and the contacts, it'd make light and shade as well, wouldn't it? It would make even the dull bits interesting because it would be 'little do they know' all the time. I mean, take the dull bits in a thriller, bits where a character walks down the road or has a cup of tea or prunes his roses, you're on tenterhooks, aren't you, the whole time? Why? Because he's getting away with it, he's got the laugh on people and he still gets his roses pruned, doesn't he? I wouldn't object to a double life because I think I've got an aptitude for it, just like some people have got an eye for a ball. Now Lola would never understand that. She'd be scandalized in all probability. It's not the sort of thing I could even talk to her about. I can't talk to her about anything without her saying that I don't love her. Tell her I've got interested in stamps or vintage cars, tell her I'm playing golf at the weekend, and what does she say? 'You don't love me.'

'Look Lo, I explained. When I phoned I told you I had a working breakfast this morning, eight fifteen. If I'd driven home it'd have been past two before I got in and then I'd have to be up by a quarter of six to be safe. And I need my eight hours. Quite apart from the fact that I don't like driving late. You know what it's like when you've had a couple of gins.'

'No, strangely enough. I've never had the chance.'

39

'Well, you can imagine. It's not that I'll have an accident. I learned to hold my liquor when I was at sea, but it's a hellish strain all the same—'

'I'm not asking you to drive when you're drunk, when you've had one too many, I'm not asking you to do that.'

'Lo, I'm sorry, but that is what you're asking. You're not suggesting that I sit there and drink lemonade are you?'

'I'm not suggesting anything.'

'But you are. That's just what you are doing. Or why did you ask about when the pubs closed? Now, come on.'

'You don't love me.'

Now here's one of those cases, one of those cases that seem to come up over and over again. I can tell she wants to cry, she wants to fly out at me, she wants to be emotional about this thing, it's obvious, isn't it? Now if I go on am I being cruel or am I being honest? Is it cruelty to want to make her see that she's being totally unreasonable? How can we keep up this place, keep things up the way we're managing if I'm not allowed to do my job? Why shouldn't she be made to see that it's more than a question of what I do when I'm out with business people, that it's impossible to live the way she seems to want me to live, thinking only of her, thinking only how to please and at the same time being responsible for a family? It's more than a question of emotion or cruelty, it's a fundamental issue, only if I go on about it I'm being unnecessary. How do you reconcile that? You don't, and when you don't you become strangers, you simply become strangers. You're closer to a stranger in a bar (I'm not talking about sex now) than you are to people you live with because you can be straight with strangers but with people you live with you're always running away and hiding, taking refuge in silence, as if silence was neutral, but it isn't, it's poisonous, it generates poisonous thoughts, it makes you want to kill people.

'Look Lo, I'm sorry but I wish I understood—'

'Home twenty minutes and you're trying to pick a quarrel, what's the matter with you? I don't see you for forty-eight hours and half an hour after you come back you're trying to pick a quarrel.'

'I want you to understand something, that's all. I don't want a quarrel. What do I want a quarrel for?'

'I suppose you were frustrated at work or something and you want to take it out on me. I'm sorry but that's how I feel about it. I look forward to you coming back—'

'O.K., I'm sorry, we won't discuss it any more. Finish. I won't mention it again. Next time I'm asked—'

'Oh do what you like, I don't mind. You don't understand anything.'

'Then explain it to me. If I don't understand, explain it to me. That's all I asked in the first place.'

'I was just thinking your duties seem a lot more fun than mine.'

'What're you talking about?'

'I mean having drinks with people, steak houses. I mean your duties seem a lot more fun than mine, that's all.'

'What duties do you have?'

'What duties do I have? Are you serious? Have you ever heard of making beds, cleaning floors, washing dishes, cooking meals—'

'Washing dishes, I said I'd get you a machine, soon as I see this bloke again from Middlesex Electric, as soon as I see him again—'

'Oh I don't care about the dishes.'

'If you want to have a gin while you're doing the dishes, why don't you?'

'What makes you think I don't?'

'What do you want of me? What in hell do you want of me frankly? I'd like to know.'

'No you wouldn't. Anyway I don't want anything from you.'

'If you're drinking by yourself, drinking on your own like that, something must be wrong and I'd like to know what it is.'

'Life.'

'Well there's always a cure for that, isn't there? Christ, I'm only joking, Lo, I'm only joking. I must say if it tastes as good as it smells it's been worth waiting for.'

'We do our best when the master deigns to come home.'

'Oh come on, Lo, knock that off. Better angry than sarcastic. Come here. Come here.'

'Stop it, Charlie, it's hot.'

'What is?'

'The dish.'

'The dish? Is it now?'

'You are vulgar.'

'What do you mean vulgar? I hope it is though after all this time, I must say.'

'It's only three days.'

'What is?'

'Since we— you are awful. No, you are, awful.'

42

'Awful am I? In what way?'
'Vulgar.'

Now look, you see? She turns away, she fiddles about with the lid of the damned casserole, she licks her fingers, she frowns. Why does she run away all the time? Why doesn't she come to me now, now, when we both bloody want it, when we're both in the mood? Because the dinner'd get cold. Would it? And whose dinner is it anyway? David might come in. David might come in and see his mother with her knickers on the ground, well then David could clear off again, couldn't he, and it'd give him something to think about next time he's fisting himself and can't think of anything better. Is that disgusting? Is that disgraceful? Well I don't give a fuck, I don't give a fuck. Who's she playing the bloody hostess for, who's she trying to please? What could be better than to shaft her right here on the dining-room floor, over the table if you like, with the dinner hot and waiting? Let the damned dinner wait. All these books that tell you about love and marriage, they're all bullshit, aren't they, crap, aren't they? Because they never tell you what to do when sex and life meet, when it's sex or the bloody casserole, they never deal with reality. Books! She reads a bit from the library, but I don't read much nowadays. I don't get the time, driving myself, except for the odd paperback, and then I go mainly for practical handbooks and spy stuff. I go quite a bit on spy stuff. I'd give a lot to know how it would damage David to see me and Lo at it. O.K., it might shock him out of his socks, O.K., but then what? Would he become impotent, would he want to jam it in himself, what would it do to him? It seems to me that you mess kids up whatever you do, you make a mess of it, it's all rigged to beat you, isn't it? You can't do the right thing, so what the hell? O.K., I never saw too much of my old man, I never had any trouble with my old woman, she did everything for me she could think of, I recognize that, I recognize that very well, but I didn't care for her, I never did. I got round her, I knew how to get things out of her but I never caught myself loving her. I was crafty. I looked like I loved her. She thought I loved her and I assume she loved me. And what effect has it all had on me? Am I awful? Am I any worse than anyone else? Not from what I read, I mean the things I read in the papers, the things I hear. How could I have been better? By loving my mother? By hurting her? By seeing more of my father? By doing what? It occurs to me now that perhaps my father and my mother didn't get on. Maybe he wasn't always away working. Maybe they actually parted for a time. Maybe that's why I'm an only child, because they decided they didn't much care for each other once they'd had me. I don't know. And if I did know, what difference would it make? I mean what would I be like if I was O.K., if everything had gone exactly according to plan, and whose plan would it have gone according to? In the end you wonder does it make any difference what we do? I've met people claim to have seen incredible things, you hear things at sea in particular you wouldn't believe, but you can hear them anywhere if you keep your ears open, if you read between the lines in the papers. What's so special about seeing people having it away? I don't say it's right, I don't say it ought to be encouraged, but what's so unbelievably awful about it? Isn't it true in a way that even when you're having it away yourself you're watching yourself at the

44

same time? How often are you completely lost in it, how often are you completely satisfied by it, I mean just by doing it, and how often do you top it off, so to speak, with the excitement of knowing that you're doing it, copping a look at yourself doing it? How often are you the same as your experience? Not often, not very often. What I'm saying is, we hide things from each other that don't mean as much as we think they do. People see other people burned alive, they see other people tortured, they see Christ knows what and they come home and lead what they call a normal life, so what's going to happen if a kid sees his mum and dad on the job? Is the ceiling going to fall in? Is that kid of mine so bloody pure as it is, is he having such lovely thoughts as it is? Is he fuck! I'm not saying it's not worth behaving decently, I'm not saying I'm in favour of family orgies or any of that sort of thing, I'm just saying that the excuses people make for not doing what they want to do because of some outside chance that something will happen, well, it's no different from my mother not daring to walk across the grass in case she got summonsed. So, I sit here and cool my casserole (it wouldn't have hurt to cool it for ten minutes, you don't need that long for a quick ram, not like the way we were both feeling) and there's Lo with her tasting face on, elbows just off the table, knees together and I couldn't say anything to her without her being disgusted or dishonest. I know as sure as I know anything she was ready for it but would she admit it now? Of course she wouldn't. And why not? Because of all those damned books she reads and all those magazines, oh it's more than that, it's English history, it's everything. Two people under their own roof, both wanting it and not daring to, and why? English history. It makes you want to see everything smashed up. It makes you want to break out and blow up the whole place. It makes you wish you were a beast. It makes me wish I was one anyway. I'd like to rip her clothes off and fuck her silly on that bloody tufted nylon carpet they swore wouldn't spot and has got more spots on it than a teenager who doesn't know where to put it. No, it's not a question of being a beast, it's a question of honesty. It's a question of making her admit what she wants as much as I do. Get her really going, old Lo, and there's no one like her; I could swallow her like an oyster I fancy her so much sometimes and yet there she is, saying I'm awful. Awful? I'm not so awful.

'What would you do if your wife was having an affair?'

'You know what I caught David doing this afternoon when he was supposed to be doing his homework?'
'All healthy boys do it.'
'Reading one of those magazines. If you can call it reading.'
'You are a prude sometimes, aren't you, Lo?'
'Have you seen them?'
'Of course I've seen them. What magazine was it exactly?'
'I don't know. They all look the same to me. A prude because I don't like those magazines? I think they're disgusting. If that's being a prude—'
'Well, isn't it?'
'We're not all like you. I don't know where he gets them.'
'He gets them at the stationer's, he gets them where every-

one else gets them. Boys like looking at pictures of naked girls, always have, always will.'

'He's thirteen. Thirteen. Did you look at pictures of naked girls when you were thirteen?'

'I did if I got the chance. The old *Lilliput*. That was the only place I knew where you could find them.'

'You would. I wonder about you sometimes. They oughtn't to sell those magazines to children.'

'You've got a short memory, Lo. Of what it was to be a kid. People don't think of themselves as children when they're thirteen. Anyway it's part of his education, part of growing up. The best part if you ask me.'

'It's—'

'What?'

'Nothing.'

'What were you going to say? What're you crying about? What is there to cry about?'

'It doesn't matter who we are does it?'

'I don't get you.'

Two people eating supper, eating casserole of beef, carrots and onions, an evening in March, is it cold, is it hot, what's been happening in the world, will the Russians and have the Americans and what does England matter any more, an evening in early June, a spring evening, an autumn evening, nights drawing in, a nip in the air, that old joke, where's the summer gone, was it on a Tuesday or a Wednesday summer this year, we don't seem to have a summer any more, salad on the table because it's only September after all and celery in a glass and it's the Chinese I'm worried about. Do you know the price of steak? Do

47

you know how much you have to pay for steak, a little piece of rump? How do people afford it? That window's tapping again. That draught-resistant strip, I don't know it doesn't seem to do any good. There's still a draught in here. I've had the man in twice. I can feel it on my knee, can't you? What about double glazing? Do you know what double glazing costs? A man called today. I reckon it's cheaper to buy a new house. Have you heard about that man bought a new house and it fell down ten days later? Fell down. Ten days later. A new house. You like fried fish, don't you? You didn't have fish for lunch did you because — sitting there all the year round, summer and winter, cold lamb, pork's reasonable this week, Irish stew, you like dumplings, don't you? You always used to like dumplings. You used to like everything. You used to eat anything I put in front of you. What about seeing the doctor? I wish you'd see the doctor. You ought to see the doctor. It's not fair. This room needs doing. The sitting-room needs doing. Have you seen the stair carpet? Have you seen how the stair carpet's wearing? When did we have that stair carpet done? It's disgraceful. I called the man and you know what he said. It's all very well for you. That's your opinion. I don't want anything for myself. I'm thinking about the children.

'It doesn't matter who you are, that's what I'm saying. He isn't ours, David. We don't matter, not really, all the trouble we take, I take, none of it matters. That magazine matters more to him than I do, more than you do.'

'Human nature isn't it? It's built into him isn't it? You can't blame him.'

'Those magazines – and the prices, where does he get the money?'

'Cost a bomb, I know. I agree with you there. It's wicked.'

'Where does he get it from? I suppose you buy them too.'

'I have done. Do you want me to lie to you? I have bought them, yes, at times.'

'I shall never understand men. I don't know why they bother to live with women at all. I don't know why they don't just sit and read magazines all the time, I really don't, and save themselves the trouble of having to keep wives and pay rent – pay mortgages –'

'I suppose that's true enough. A lot of blokes, if they were honest, I reckon they'd just as soon have things organized on completely different principles –'

'And how do you think we feel, women?'

'I think you feel marvellous as I was trying to demonstrate before this casserole came between us.'

'I don't mean that and well you know it.'

'Oh Christ I'm only trying – you don't want me to talk to you, do you?'

'What would you do if your wife was having an affair?'

'What would I do? Depend whether I knew about it or not wouldn't it?'

'Assuming you knew about it?'

'I don't know.'

'It doesn't honestly occur to you she might, does it? You take her for granted to such a degree it doesn't even occur to you. Why shouldn't she have an affair if she wants to?'

49

'I never said she shouldn't. You asked me what I'd do about it.'

'Well, what would you do about it? Don't tell me you wouldn't do anything.'

'I never said that. I don't know what I'd do.'

'You know what I think? I think you're despicable. And a liar. I think you're a low form of life.'

'And what do you think you are?'

'You'd go out of your mind. You'd half kill her. You wouldn't let her go, would you?'

'Let her go? Go where?'

'With this man she was having an affair with. You'd fight tooth and nail to stop her, wouldn't you?'

'All you ever do is get angry.'

'I'm not angry.'

'Of course you are, you always are, whenever I say anything.'

'I'm not angry with you. I'm angry, if I'm angry at all, with the way we pretend all the time.'

'You pretend as much as anyone. And pretend what?'

'I don't necessarily deny that. Pretend – as if someone was watching us, as if we were being judged all the time and had to – well, pretend – pretend that – oh that we wouldn't ever dream – dream of *anything* – that we're absolutely made for each other twenty-four hours a day. You know as well as I do.'

'I know very well it wouldn't matter to you who you lived with –'

'Do you know what my father said when I told him I was getting married? Do you know what he said? He said just that, more or less, he said I don't think it much matters who you marry, you can marry anyone really, it doesn't make much odds what woman you marry.'

'He's never liked me.'

'You didn't come into it. He didn't mean anything against you. He meant people aren't anything like as unique as we all like to think, that's all. You can rub along with most anyone as long as, you know. He likes you, who said he didn't?'

'We never see him anyway. Marrying again like that—'

'I'm damned glad he did. Saves him coming round here all the time, which would have been the alternative. Why shouldn't he marry again? She's not a bad woman.'

'Half his age.'

'No point in marrying someone double your age is there?'

'She's not much more than a tart and you know it.'

'I've known some quite decent tarts. She looks after him, she looked after him when he had that operation, and she works hard. I don't think she's a tart.'

'I'll bet you have known some tarts. I bet you have.'

'Look for Christsake I was at sea for three years, what do you think I am, a saint?'

'I don't know what you wanted to get married for.'

'Look don't be bloody silly. You want me to lie, don't you? That's what you want.'

She lived with her mother. She lived with her mother in Ongar; mother was a civil servant and they had this flat over a newsagent's. She did secretarial work at the local hospital. One day I was supposed to play golf, I'd got quite keen on it during shore leaves, it was always something I thought I could do, play golf. The cottage we took down in Suffolk, there was a sack of old clubs there, hickory shafts, rusted blades, but I used to hack around with them in the field, the field with the yellow flowers it must have been, and a couple of balls I cadged off the links near by, stole I suppose you'd say, watch people drive I used to, and then I'd nip on to the fairway and away before they could catch up with me. I never took those people seriously as people, they were just distant figures swinging their clubs up on the chair over the tenth, I only considered they were there to give me a chance to nick some balls. Anyway, back to Lo; I'd made this arrangement to play golf with a mate of mine and it came on to rain, they were chucking it down, you couldn't set foot outside without getting drenched, so there we were and he had this van, rackety old thing, but it went, he worked in the shore office, Michael, his name was, Michael Gage. He had an Austin van with windows fitted in the back, fitted them himself, not that brilliantly as a matter of fact, but there it was; it had wheels and it went. Well we thought if there was no golf we might as well go to the pictures, see what was on, a Thursday afternoon, bloody miserable afternoon, March or April, and we went into this newsagent and there was Lo. Nineteen, twenty she must have been, red hair, freckles, with this funny frown on her face, touching really it was, this lopsided frown. I assumed it was her place but it turned out later she was helping because the lady had—phlebitis could it have been? She had something wrong with her and she'd had to go into hospital. As soon as you get involved with people health seems to come into it. I asked did she work in the place, you know what two blokes are like when they get a girl on their own, a lot more forth-coming, a lot more cheeky if you like, than when you're on

your own. When you're on your own you can't think what
to say, but two blokes together, it's a different thing entirely.
I remember two shipmates of mine, they always used to
find a prossy that'd do the two of them together, take 'em
both on. I was dead shocked when they told me. I didn't say
so, but I was. I thought it sounded terrible, shooting off
with another bloke on the job at the same time, I thought
there was something immoral about it. It was what they liked
doing, that was all, and if the price was right the woman
wasn't grumbling. What was I being so bloody moral about
I wonder? I was like Lo. Now I don't want to give the
wrong impression, she wasn't prim or anything like that,
she wasn't above a bit of flirtation and she had on this
jumper I remember, terrible purple colour, home-made
looking and you could see she had a decent pair on her all
right. Notice how when two men talk to a girl with a good
pair on her one talks to her face and the other one concen-
trates on her knockers? I've seen it time and again. Well, we
chatted her up, went on at her, half an hour we must've
been in there. Would she come out with us? Did she have a
friend, all that kind of stuff? Dead common, I'm not denying
it. I didn't think about it at the time and in view of what
came later you may think I'm trying to put a good face on
it, but even while we were talking to her in this deliberate,
cheeky lower-deck manner, I remember thinking, because I
can see the bottles of sweets against the sunshine (just our
luck it'd stopped raining when the course was under water
and it was real April sunshine, rainbows everywhere and the
shop was full of dust and that smell of rain like the whole
world's had a good wash), I remember I thought this isn't
me talking like this to this girl, and it's not this girl listening

53

and frowning against us and the sun, neither of us is being ourselves, it's all rubbish and yet on we went, wasn't there anything she liked better than serving sweets and hadn't she got any sweets that weren't on show, we bet she had and all that business, people coming into the shop all the time and we'd wait our turn again and buy a few gob-stoppers and find a silly joke to make every time and she'd say 'Please' in a hurt, amused voice and we'd say 'Thank *you*' it makes me blush to think of it now. And then in the end of course she didn't have a friend, at least not one she was going to throw to a couple of layabouts like we must've seemed and she was busy herself (as if she'd come out with us!) and we were on the pavement and climbing into this runty little van and screaming away over the wet road. I can't remember what we did that night, pictures probably or a dance hall, I don't remember. Next leave I had I bought myself a little car, I had some pay saved and this bloke was emigrating and he sold me a Ford Anglia, not a bad little banger, bit rusty and lopsided but it went along all right. He told me that blokes who wanted to be racing drivers bought these little Fords because they were the nearest thing to sports car performance you could get, just right for the next best thing to Handsome, he said, cheeky sod. Anyway I bought it, eighty quid and I had to invest in a set of new tyres. Well, as chance would have it, and that really is true because I never gave this girl a thought between the time we walked out of the shop and this next leave I had, it must have been a good four months, I remember it was full summer because they were playing cricket on the green across from the shop, four months later I found myself passing these links where Mickey Gage and I had been supposed to play and that made me think of the girl. When I saw the shop I thought I was going to be sick, I was so, well I was so moved honestly. My heart was banging in the back of my throat I thought I was going to fetch up my lunch, some rotten pie I'd had, and I couldn't decide what to do, I was like a kid. I was shaking. I got out of the car and I paced up and down, I was like sixteen. And it wasn't as if I hadn't known a few women, I'd known a few women, only I was shaking, just like I was sixteen years old and about to ask my first girl to some bloody awful hop. What was it all about? I mean, I know it was about Lola, about this girl I didn't even know her name, but why fear? Why *fear*? Anyway, of course finally in I went and she wasn't there, she was at work. I hung around all day, I hung around, I couldn't do anything, couldn't even be bothered to go and play golf, I practised a bit and a bloke offered me a game but I thought no, it'll take too long. You can take three and a half hours to go round some of these courses. She was due back about half five, so ten past I'm walking casually up and down because I've got to catch her as she comes along, otherwise she'll be up in the flat and that'll be that. Finally I see her getting off the bus across the way. I'm so nervous I try to persuade myself it isn't her. I try to tell myself that it can't be as simple as that, that she's been delayed or she's meeting someone straight from work and it can't be her. To tell the truth, she looks a bit less attractive if anything than I remembered, neat, clean, nicely turned out but less, well, sexy, that side of things. Here again, I swear it's true, at the same time as I thought that, I thought I shall marry this girl. It didn't seem like a blessing or a revelation or anything, it was more like going to the pictures and suddenly realizing that you know how it's going to end, a mixture between a feeling of power and disappointment, helplessness. I could have walked away, I could have let her pass, there wasn't a single reason why I had to talk to her, but as she came level with me, I said, 'Hello, fancy bumping into you.' Not very original, I admit, and I was quite ready for her to look blank and walk right past, but she smiled and said, 'Oh hello, I didn't recognize you at first,' even though it was only a second since I'd spoken, less than a second, so maybe she'd seen me before, maybe that surprised look on her face was something deliberate. How can you tell? I'm not saying she did see me before she said she did, I'm not accusing her, but I can't help wondering sometimes, I can't help wondering if I've ever really known what's going on. I said, 'This *is* a coincidence,' and she said, 'Yes,' squinting at me as if I was the sun, and the sun coming over my shoulder into her hair. 'We ought to make something of it,' I said, 'if you're not doing anything, I've got my car round the corner.' She smiled then, smiled straight at me and I smiled too and looked down, you know. 'I was going to buy a paper,' I said, 'I had a horse, I wanted to see how it'd done.' Now that was a complete fabrication because I've never cared about horses one way or the other. Anyway she nodded. I said, 'Well, what about it? Are you doing anything, tonight I mean?' 'Are you living round here then?' 'I've got a bit of leave that's all, a few days.' I might as well have proposed then. I could feel it coming that clearly. 'I'll have to fix it with mother,' she said, 'because I said I'd take her to her meeting. She's got a meeting.' 'Oh well ... ' 'No, I can probably fix it. One of her friends'll take her.' 'If you're sure – ' 'I expect it'll be all right.' 'Well then what time shall we say? Seven? That be O.K.?' 'Seven is fine.' 'I'll pick you up at seven.' When she opened the door I said, 'By the way I'm Charlie Hanson,' and she said Lola Furness and we both smiled and I was in there meeting the mother as if we'd already fixed the day. I'd never so much as held her hand. When I told her my name I remember thinking at the same time, what a let down, just having a name like that, it was like promising her I wasn't really anybody special, I thought Charlie Hanson, here I am saddling myself with you again and I never liked you, why do we have to drag you into it? Why can't you leave me be?

'Take off your sweater, do as I say.'
'I don't want to. It's cold.'
'No it's not, take it off when I tell you to. No, pull it up over your face, just pull it up over your face. Never mind taking it off.'

It's a funny thing to say, but I sometimes think marriage hasn't got anything to do with sex at all. I mean the reasons for it. You don't marry a girl because of the sex thing, even if you think you do. That first night we went out to an Indian meal, which she said she liked, and then we went to a film. I've never been so stiff in my life, and I don't mean that way, I mean I've never had such a crick in my neck. Usually you took a girl to the flicks, you settled down with a box of chocolates, to give you a good reason for huddling up close together, and then you got down to snogging, or at least creeping your arm round her and getting a feel if you could, but I couldn't do it with Lo. I sat there catching a crafty look at her profile as if she was royalty or something, looking at her hair out of the side of my eyes, as you might say, and then turning to look at this film they were showing. Why are films always so bloody awful? You hear about them and you go and they're mostly bloody awful, I don't know why. She was wearing a black suit and a white blouse with ruffles on it, these ruffles all the way down the front and patent leather shoes. I felt like I was out with a lady. She had a quiet way with her, a sort of reserve, it made you feel you'd never been out with anyone quite like it before. The fact was, being an only child and moving about the place, I never really felt at home anywhere, never had people I'd grown up with, never felt part of any place we lived in. There was always something sort of provisional about the way we lived, and this uncertainty about it, which I never realized when I was a kid but I realize it now like I realize that my mother and my old man never really liked living together. It sounds ridiculous, but I more or less assumed that Lo had never even been kissed. She had this very pale skin with these freckles, you felt she'd bruise if you touched her; you'd say she probably had Irish blood and I think she did, I think she had an Irish grandfather. I didn't so much as touch her that night, we got to her doorstep and I hadn't so much as touched her, unless you count her elbow leaving the Kohinoor to go to the cinema. And I wasn't exactly crazy to either, I wasn't mad for her or anything, and yet I wanted to see her again; I'd've done anything to see her again. She made me feel very inadequate, apologetic, without meaning to in any way, at the restaurant for instance and my hands, I hated the way my hands had got being at sea, I didn't like to have them show because she had very white hands herself, very delicate looking and orange nails, she wore a pale orange nail varnish I'd never seen anything quite like it and it did something for her eyes, she had green eyes and this orange nail varnish, I reckon I did fancy her, but not to get a hard on for, not directly like that, she made me feel too uncertain for that. I thought if I could have her I'd be something, it'd give me something to live up to. How do you end up wanting to kill a woman like that? Not that I do all the time, it's just this little secret of mine, this secret way out, this imaginary emergency exit. Killing her, it's like marrying her, I don't want to do it, I don't hate her, I don't think of it with pleasure, but it seems the only way. Anyway, I said, 'What about tomorrow?' and she said, 'Tomorrow's a bit difficult,' vaguely, like a head waiter looking round to see if he can find you a table, nothing personal in it, just a question of availability, but I knew we would see each other again, difficult or not, and soon, because on this first date of ours she asked me a lot of questions and told me a lot about herself, about her school and her background, about how her old man had gone and left her mum and then got killed in an accident soon after he'd agreed to come back. Somehow I felt as if we'd had the same parents, even though there wasn't really much similarity, I felt as if I understood, even though – and this sounds like a terrible confession – even though I was bored to death listening to her, listening to her telling me about how she'd nearly got this job in Denver, I think it was, in Denver, Colorado, only she hadn't got one of the languages they wanted, in America. *One* of the languages, Jesus, I felt like an ignoramus, a complete ignoramus. And yet now I tell her something and she can't remember who people are I told her about yesterday. It's as if another woman had been substituted for her at the last moment, like in those shops you get in places like Gib and Tangier and Naples where they wrap up what you think you've bought and when you unwrap it a thousand miles away it's something half as good and you've paid the original price. When a woman tells you her past, you can be sure she intends you to be her future, you can quote me there. The next date we had she said we shouldn't go out to eat, it was silly, we could have something at her place. I never expected her mother as well. We had her mother there right through the meal, it was quite good I must say, this fricassee of chicken, she'd taken a lot of trouble, but her mother was sitting there with us right through the meal. I was very polite, actually, I was amazed how polite I was, making conversation with this old woman. As a matter of fact she was quite interesting, she knew quite a lot, she worked in the Admiralty at one time and she was quite well up on ships and the sea and I could tell she was making a big effort, as if she'd been tipped off, which no doubt she had. All the same the thought of the whole evening in this flat with Lo and her mother it would have made you want to go and see anything that was showing, musical, foreign picture, anything, anything, bloody awful or not, even something about love. I hadn't even got a paper and it was getting late; if we didn't go soon we'd be too late and then this old woman, she gets up and says, 'Heavens I must be going!' and Lola said, 'Mother's going to a meeting.' This old woman she must've gone to a meeting every night. She was like a quick change artist, one minute she was sitting there screwed to the floor and the next she had her hat on and her outdoor coat and she was saying, 'Turn the gas off when you got out,' and 'Nice to meet you,' and there was the front door banging. Lola was

60

in the kitchen washing up and I sat in the window and looked at last week's local paper. They had some books, but I can never bring myself to look at books at times like that, so I sat there turning over this out-of-date paper. Lola came in, wiping her hands, smiling, and she said, 'I thought she'd never go,' and I said, 'I never knew she was meaning to.' You don't think I'd subject you to a whole evening of mother do you?' And I said, 'Oh I wouldn't have minded, she's very nice,' and do you know I meant it in a funny way? As soon as she was gone, I thought she wasn't a bad sort. 'What're these meetings she goes to?' 'Oh well, sometimes it's bridge and sometimes it's the W.I. and sometimes I don't know.' 'I suppose those are the ones she enjoys,' I said, and she looked down and I saw she was blushing and I thought Christ if she doesn't smile in a moment I'll be out and then she looked up and she was smiling and throwing her hair back and giving me this squint. I said, 'Pictures or what?' and she said, 'I don't mind about the pictures, we can always watch the TV if you like,' and I said, 'Doesn't matter to me.' She said, 'We've got the place to ourselves.' I should've been pleased I suppose but I felt a sort of panic when she said that, I thought what can we talk about, what'll we do all evening? It never occurred to me, I swear, that we'd do what we did. She said, 'Would you mind helping me in the kitchen?' and I thought, Christ here we go, I'm drying up and acting the tame monkey, we might as well be married, only I haven't got a blind thing out of it. So we go into the kitchen and there are all the dishes stacked up and everything shipshape, except not put away. 'They go in the top cupboard, so if you wouldn't mind passing them up.' I could've reached but she was hopping on a chair before I could budge so I started passing them up. It was strange, I was passing these plates up to her without a thought, staring out of the window onto this arterial road and a junction where cars coming in had to slow down and I looked up at her and she was on tiptoe with the last plate and it sounds funny but what really excited me suddenly was her foot lifting just a little way out of her shoe. She wasn't wearing stockings and the tendon was stretched and her heel was just clear of the shoe and Christ I could've grabbed her. I didn't though, I thought she'd go mad, so I reckon I must've scowled, I must've looked annoyed because she frowned down at me then, brushing her hair back, and she said 'Something wrong?' 'No,' I said, 'why?' 'The way you looked I thought perhaps—' and she held out her hand, as if she always did, held out her hand, not even looking at me, and I took it and she hopped off the chair and I stood back to let her land and she stumbled and she was in my arms and I opened my mouth to apologize, I was just about to apologize when she was pressing her face against me and turning her mouth back and forth across mine and moaning like she'd just had some bad news and I said, 'Hullo—' but I couldn't say more because she was pressing herself against me and kissing me, well, I had a lot to do to catch up with her, I kissed her back and she was bumping against me like a tug in a high wind and moaning, her eyes shut, I was quite alarmed, that may sound funny, but I was, I was afraid there was something wrong with her. Sometimes now she says to me, 'It wouldn't matter who I was,' well that was how I felt. When she'd finished kissing—and I had my tongue in her mouth and everything by that time—she suddenly blinked and stood off and said, 'Do you want coffee?' Just like that, as if none of it had ever happened. I said, 'Just as you like,' so she made coffee. Took hours, and then she brought it in and we looked at the *Radio Times* which was all there was in those days and sipped this coffee which was so hot you could hardly touch the cup and I thought well I suppose that was it because I couldn't believe we'd ever get back to where we'd just been, it was as if it had never happened. She took the cups and put them on the sideboard and then she turned on the telly and we sat on the leather sofa, plastic I suppose it was, and watched some parlour game, television was all parlour games in those days, we watched this parlour game not touching or anything and she turned to me after a bit and said, 'Rather good isn't it?' and I thought rather good, it's the worst load of rubbish I ever saw in my life, these women jangling their bracelets and smiling, and people clapping all the time, I thought it was a complete load of rubbish. Anyway, we sat there watching it and finally she said, 'You don't like it do you?' and I said, 'It's all right,' like you always do and she smiled and got up and went over to the windows, it was still quite light outside and drew the curtains. Then she came back and turned off the box and sat down again and I thought well this is it so I pushed her back into the corner and began to kiss her again and right away there we were again, only this time she was staring at me so hard I almost had to stop and then I saw that her blouse was sort of out of the top of her skirt and I could see her slip and then she might have been anyone, you know, and I started to unbutton her blouse and I was waiting for her to stop me only she didn't and there she was with her blouse all open and this thick brassière on her like they wore in those days, only it was quite low at the top and I could see

63

the freckles where her breasts began, so I kissed her throat and her breastbone and that and she was all hot, this white skin was all blotched with red and hot, burning. I had hell's own time with the catch on this bra, it would've held the *Queen Mary*, and I kept thinking it's all going to come to an end, I could swear it couldn't last, I was taking bets with myself, and then suddenly the catch was undone and the bra slipped down and sure enough, though it almost seemed incredible at the time, there were her nipples, big, pink, with a few very pale hairs growing out of them and I was almost crying, I don't know why, but I could feel tears in my throat. She kept stroking my head, like she was sorry for me and here I was having myself a field day at the same time. I had such a hard on now I thought I'd split my pants and I was wondering how to get her to do something for me, because I never thought of going all the way, I hadn't even got anything with me which proves how much of a chance I thought I had because I never went anywhere normally when I was ashore without a packet and at the same time I was hoping that she'd stop me because I was worried about what might happen. Meanwhile of course I had my hand on her knee and I was thinking this time she'll shut up shop for sure and her knees were tight and just for politeness I knocked again and Christ she was open and I had my hand all the way up and that was it I couldn't stop then, only I had to get off her a bit to get my things down and I looked at her and she was lying there with her eyes half closed and the lids swollen like she'd been crying and her breasts open and I suppose I knew then they wouldn't last, I knew they were the kind'd go soft when she had a kid, though don't ask me how I knew. She might have been drugged or half dead or something, in the middle of an operation and her skin was white again, no sign of the pink there'd been there before, and her belly moving slightly, but only slightly as if she was dying and I was quite panicky in case she started to cry or turn away because I knew I wouldn't be able to do anything for her, I knew I'd have to leave her to sort herself out, I'd probably just walk out, I thought, if she started but in the meanwhile I had my things off. She turned slightly and her tits moved and they were like twin animals, blind twin animals and I was down petting them again and I was thinking at the same time this can't last and what am I going to do, I knew a lot of blokes withdrew, that was the only precaution they took, but I wondered if there'd be time, and I had my hands up her skirt again, it was all twisted around, and I thought this is it because she suddenly gave a great heave and sort of pushed me away and I thought that's it, curtains, only all she did was she pulled down the zip and sort of lifted herself up and there she was with the skirt on the floor. So I had her there on the sofa and she came on so strong I couldn't stop myself, if I'd pulled it out I think she would've thumped me; so I didn't and that was David.

'Marriage has to be give and take, doesn't it? There has to be give and take.'
'That's right. You give and she takes.'

I said, 'Don't worry, I'll give up the sea.'
And she said, 'No, I don't want you to give anything up for me.'
'It wouldn't be for you, it'd be for us,' I said, but I was so bloody depressed it can't have sounded very convincing.

We were sitting on a park bench near the cemetery, there was this bit of park outside the cemetery with almond trees or something all cut so short, pruned so short you felt uncomfortable, as if they must be in pain with it, like bitten fingernails, and there was a dusty wind blowing, this hot wind, dusty, made you sneeze, just like that wind across the field with the yellow flowers. 'I don't like it that much anyway, I was thinking of giving it up anyway, getting a steady job, it's not that much of a life, honestly, the sea.'

'I wish I knew someone,' she said, and her face was all blotchy, she looked more like nine months than ten days or whatever it was, ten days overdue that is.

I said, 'You don't want to do anything like that,' thinking why the hell don't you go and do it, you must know someone, of course you must, working in a hospital, only I couldn't say it. I was impatient because all along I knew we were going to get married. Why couldn't she admit it, though, that she had me on a hook, instead of pretending?

She said, 'You don't want to marry me.'

I said, 'Look, Lo, what's the point in saying a thing like that? We're as good as married already.' I meant it bitterly, but it must've sounded different because she gave me this lovely smile, tears all over her face, and she bent and she kissed my hands. She took my hands and she kissed them, as if it was my cock or something she was kissing, as if she meant something very intimate by it, and there were these women sitting with their prams and their bags of oranges and their knitting and she was kissing my fingers.

Suddenly she said, 'Charlie, there's something I haven't told you, something I want to tell you.'

I thought, Christ, twins; but she went on kissing my

fingers, studying the callouses and that, they were so cracked I couldn't never really get them clean, I said, 'My hands didn't used to be like that.'

She said, 'I love them, I love them,' and she was crying and kissing me and all these women chucking their peel at the litter bins and missing and I felt half mad; I wasn't in love I didn't think, I wasn't hot for her, I was dead choked over the whole business, but I knew I was going to marry her and I knew something terribly important was happening to me, something I wasn't equal to but I knew it was happening. I thought all the time I was letting her down, like something was being asked of me I couldn't deliver, and she said, 'It's about my father.'

'I thought he was dead.'

'He is dead,' she said, 'only it wasn't an accident.'

'Wasn't an accident?'

'No,' she said, 'he was murdered.'

Well, I don't know what difference that was supposed to make to anything but I felt like I'd been stung by a hornet. I thought, Christ where's it going to end? All I said was, 'What do you mean murdered?' as if murdered was a word in a language I'd never heard before.

'Murdered. He was murdered. Some people killed him.'

'Who? And why?' And what the hell do I care, I wanted to ask her, and why bother to tell me, as if this had anything to do with us, and at the same time I felt that she was right and it did have something to do with us and that what was more it was, which it obviously wasn't, something she ought to be ashamed of, something that made her seem other than she'd seemed before, less. Something if she'd told me sooner we'd never have got involved in all this.

'Well, we don't know that he was murdered—'

Christ, make up your mind. 'Suppose you tell me about it.' Inspector Hanson here.

'— he was supposed to have quarrelled with some men over some scrap metal and he was driving home in his van and the steering went, at least that's what they think, and he went into a lorry.'

'No one ever proved it was murder then?'

'No one ever proved it, no, but the police told mother they thought someone *had* tampered with the van, only they'd never be able to prove it.' I thought, you little bitch, don't ask me why but I did, I thought you little whore, I thought terrible things, I don't know why. I was so ashamed feeling what I did I found myself saying all kinds of nice things to her. And already I felt she'd got clean away from me, I'd never known her, and her tits were already marked off for the kid. I never enjoyed them the same way again, not like I had that night in the flat.

I remember saying to her later on, 'Why did you tell me that about your old man that day outside the cemetery?' and she said, 'I don't know, only I just suddenly felt I had to tell you.' 'But what for?' 'I don't know. I thought if I didn't tell you then I'd never be able to tell you.' 'I realize that, only what would it've mattered? I'm not saying it wouldn't've mattered, but can you tell me why, I mean what does it really have to do with you? That's what I'd like to know. Simply as a matter of information.' 'I had a feeling,' she said, 'I don't know what exactly, I had a feeling that maybe you thought too highly of me. I didn't want you to think that I was anything too special, too grand, that's how I felt.' I respect what she did, only unfortunately it didn't have the desired effect, because all that happened, now I think about it, is that she sort of split. She didn't just become a different person, she became two different people, one the same as the girl I first met, cool and untouchable and a bit too grand for me and I resented that in a way and the other one something almost without a face that had no right to be so, so — ordinary, I mean to be so sure of herself, and her I resented in a different way, because I thought how dare she be so certain of herself.

'You can't leave her like that, she can't breathe properly. It's inhuman.'
'So?'

So anyway we got married. I had one more trip to make, I'd more or less said I would and I thought we could do with the money, because I'd looked around a bit but I hadn't fixed on anything definite. I told her we should get married before I went so she wouldn't have to worry. She said, 'I wouldn't worry.' I said, 'You might, you might think I'd never come back, you know what sailors are, you might easily think that,' and she said, 'What do you think I am, as if I would?' But I reckon she did think exactly that and when we did get married in a great mess of other people's soggy confetti, I still felt as if she'd not trusted me, as if she'd forced me into it, whereas in fact I'd forced myself into it at least as much. It was a bloody miserable occasion, however you look at it, that wedding, with two mother-in-laws and no men except me and Mick Gage and then I felt as if I was a fool. He was the one who talked to her tits when we chatted her up in the sweetshop and I felt as if I'd been landed and he'd had the fun, as if he was the one who put her in the club and I was paying the subscription. I never spoke to him again. When he kissed the bride I was that choked I thought I would go and thump someone or something; he had this little smile on his face. He had very neat lips, Mickey, almost like a woman, cupid's bow kind of thing, and it gave him this sly look. He kept smiling at me and I could've clipped him honestly, afterwards, drinking champagne with those old women. I felt like she wasn't worth the licence, poor old Lola, even though she didn't show at all and she had a nice new dress. I hated wearing that stupid bloody carnation and having a car with a driver and a white ribbon on it; all I could think was, Christ, trapped. We had a bit of a honeymoon in a caravan a friend of Mickey's lent us actually because we wanted to save as much as we could and it seemed a good way. We never had it again as good as that first time on the sofa. It wasn't the caravan, it was one of those big permanent type ones, on a site, and it had quite a decent bed. The first night she put on a nightie and I thought here we go. I couldn't say anything, but I reckoned she was trying to be something she wasn't really, proper, and I remembered how wet she was to my fingers that first night and I thought, right. I hated how she'd taken so much trouble, and all she was doing was trying to please me I suppose. She kept talking, saying how nice it was and how glad she was it was just the two of us and I couldn't think anything but shut up and grab hold of me, you bitch, why don't you, and she was sighing away and holding my hand. The thing was, she wanted to be my wife, I suppose, she wanted it to *mean* something and to me it didn't mean more than the end of something. I wasn't getting away with anything any more.

70

I didn't feel like I was scoring before the kick-off which is really getting ahead of the game, I didn't feel young any more. The opposite. After the honeymoon, I went on this last trip I'd said I'd do. We parted good friends, there weren't any quarrels or anything like that. I'd got her to do a few things, and I know this sounds bad, but when I got her to do things I was sure she'd never done before, when I turned her into a stranger again, someone I didn't entirely know, someone I wasn't entirely responsible for, then I wanted her again like I had that night on the sofa after her mother'd gone out. I wanted her because she wasn't afraid exactly, but trembling, on the verge of wanting something she wanted and feared at the same time, then I was excited too and wanted her like I had before. But I was worried too, because I was married to her; I wouldn't have worried if she'd just been a bint I'd picked up, but married to a woman and only wanting her when I'd turned her into a stranger again, that was queer, it worried me that, because it meant I'd have to keep turning her into a stranger and myself into one too, if we were to go on wanting each other.

'We could promise.'

This last trip, it took in Amsterdam again, I suppose subconsciously maybe I wanted to have one last bash, anyway when we'd finished and got paid off, some of the lads got together and we were off up Newdike, which was good for a laugh to start with, including this pair who liked to have a woman between them, only somehow this never used to come out, this thing they had, until we'd had a few beers and then it was always a kind of surprise, as if we'd never heard of it before, and even between them it was the same, they sort of had to gear themselves up to admit it to each other again, even though they'd done it often enough. This bloke came into the bar and he offered to show us a few things, you know how they do, and I was telling myself it didn't make any difference, a lot of the blokes were married and they didn't worry, they figured what their wives didn't know wouldn't hurt 'em, but I couldn't get up any of the usual feeling, I felt like there was a glass panel between me and the world. I lagged behind the others out of this bar, I didn't actually mean to, so far as I know, but I did, I lagged behind, I was by myself and I could feel Lola's eyes on me, I could see her eyes and I thought, Christ she's really got the hooks in.

'Watch you? How can I watch you?'

I looked at these women sitting in their windows in their armchairs, with all kinds of fancy lighting some of them, mauve, red, lamps with coloured bulbs in them, strips of coloured fluorescent lighting some of them, and it made them look like something unreal, and there was Lo's face, that pale freckled face and her big pale tits, like they'd been that night, only they weren't sexy, they just made her look vulnerable, stripped, as if she was going to be tortured, at the mercy of something. There was one girl I used to fancy, she was very small and she used to sit in a straight chair, like a kitchen chair, in a window with just an ordinary light. I used to imagine that she was afraid, I used to imagine that she didn't really like what she was doing or that someone was threatening her, that she dreaded someone coming back

72

who was going to hurt her or knew something about her. I used to watch her from across the canal sometimes. Sometimes I'd see a man coming along towards her place, a fat bloke, or old, and I'd nip over and just get to her door before he did, though likely as not he didn't have any intention of going in, and then I'd go in and I'd smile, like I'd saved her from something and she wouldn't say anything, of course, because probably it was all in my head, you know, and I'd say was she free, smiling I'd be as if we shared this secret, and she'd look down and then she'd put the bolt across and draw the curtains and of course she wasn't any different, I suppose, from the others, and nor was I to her. There wasn't much she wouldn't do, only I liked her because she was very clean with it, her body, she always smelt clean, with a touch of scent between her tits and on her belly, I liked that. Sometimes, well once, I made her laugh; we did something and I grinned at her and she laughed and Christ I could've married her. Anyway this time I was thinking at least there's old Brenda, because that was her name, at least she said it was; if I'd told her I wanted her to be Queen Juliana she would've said she was I suppose, but she did say her name was Brenda and I was really looking forward to her because I always wanted her, she had this strange fragility and at the same time she could work a right old nutcrackers; she could get on you when things got going and Christ. I never liked just going up to a woman, even when I was crazy for it, even then I'd like to watch them for a while, I'd like to watch a woman I'd decided to have, watch her smoke a cigarette in her window, if it was Amsterdam, or walk up and down a bit, scratch her ear, do something human, and then I'd think right I'll have you. I almost preferred watching them before

73

than messing about with them once we'd got our things off. You couldn't kiss them much or anything like that, because they'd start looking at their watches sort of business, I mean not really necessarily, but they'd be fiddling with you, trying to pretend they wanted you quick but really just trying to get you to come. (A shipmate of mine had this gag he used to trot out, 'What's in a prossy's telegram?' Answer, 'Come at once.') I tell you a fancy I used to have and that was to save all my money from a couple of trips and buy one of them outright. I used to imagine going up to one and saying how much for a night, and then a week, and a month and a year, and then how much do you want for ever, I couldn't see the difference really. If a woman I was watching went with someone else I'd be quite put out sometimes, quite offended I'd be, as if she should have known. I took it quite personally. The thing I liked best was seeing a woman turn down a bloke, talk to him and then walk away, refuse to have anything further to do with him, and then I'd go up to her and I'd say what about it and of course she'd say O.K. because that was what she was there for, and she'd only have turned this other bloke down because he wanted something wasn't on her menu or he was asking to go without the rubber, which some of them, especially in this country won't do, or else he was just teasing her and hadn't got the ready, but all the same ... I'll tell you something funny; I often wondered what these blokes they turned down did want, exactly, I mean, when it wasn't a question of money. One of the girls did volunteer once that the bloke I'd seen her talking to had just whispered abuse at her, called her a this and a that, asked her this and that about prices and suchlike, but mainly he'd just wanted to call her a something something. I never

74

asked her, she volunteered it. I've often been curious about things, but I've never had the nerve to ask. I watch, but I don't ask, I can't bring myself. I don't know whether it was shyness or what it was, whether perhaps I didn't want to know they were human, like I don't want to know when Lo's got indigestion for instance or her veins are bothering her. I always used to be afraid that the girls I'd got used to seeing, whether it was in Omsterdom or anywhere else, I'd always be afraid they'd have moved, shifted their billets or just disappeared. I used to get into quite a sweat as I got near their corner and I knew I'd be looking in a minute to see if they were still there. Sometimes, of course, they weren't and then I don't know, it sounds stupid, but I'd be more than disappointed, I'd feel betrayed, unloved, I'd feel it was an unlucky night. I'd feel something personal in it. France is a funny place, Cherbourg for instance, you'd find a certain district'd be humming with prossies one time, the hotels all lit up and that, I remember one time I saw this French officer, with his swagger stick and his funny round hat, you know those hats they wear, wearing this hat and these polished boots, I thought Christ what's General de Gaulle doing here, I mean he was the opposite of what people are usually when they're around tarts, slinking around they are usually and pretending to be nobody, but this bloke he couldn't've been more obvious if he'd had an escort of the household cavalry, he'd have been conspicuous at the troop-ing of the colour, this bloke, and I thought if any of his men are around they'll cop it in the morning, but then I see him swagger up to this woman and she's one of those tarts she's almost too much, she's stacked like they'd been architect-designed, talk about defying gravity, the biggest pair I'd seen in a long time, and as this officer comes past in these boots and everything she gives him a look like she was a general and he hadn't got his cap on. Anyway he stops and he's a foot taller than she is and it's obvious they're going to have a duel to the death, you can see that, and he indicates the door of the hotel with his stick and she goes off up the stairs and he looks round the street, slaps his boot with his cane and he's up after her, un, deux, trois. I'd never have gone for a woman like that. I daresay he made her take off every stitch before he consented to so much as take off his hat, while he sat there tapping his boot, but I could never have managed it. I don't know whether it's class or money or what does that for you. When I came back another trip I did go by that place though and it wasn't there any more, only this bloody great supermarket. Unless I'm the one making the changes, they worry me, I don't like anything different unless I know about it in advance. Anyway, this last trip of mine, I went back to where this little girl had her billet and my heart was thumping, all the usual nerves, not about having her but because I was afraid she wouldn't be there. And then at the same time I was hoping she wouldn't because I was willing to take it as a sign, if she wasn't there, that it was all over, me and her, that it was in the stars. So I turn the corner, it was right on one of the big canals up from the docks, one of the ones the river buses take with all these tourists looking out and this bloke talking into his microphone and you can't help wondering what they're saying, when the windows have got all these girls in them, I suppose it's picturesque or maybe they're telling these old people about the glories of the architecture, I don't know, anyway I turn the corner and there's this smell, fresh and foul all at once, sea and sewage and electricity, a sort of blue smell, if you know what I mean, slightly salt, as if there'd been a short circuit somewhere and the thing had been repaired only there was still this tang in the air, a scorched sort of smell, and I look and she's sitting there, just as if she'd been waiting for me all the time.

'What's the difference between this woman and any other?'

I was pleased and I was upset at the same time because I thought Christ maybe I'm mad, maybe I can get out of the whole thing, out of being married, out of Lola, maybe I can cut and run while there's still time, I've married the girl, I've done the right thing by her but how can I spend the rest of my life wheeling a pram because that's what it's going to come to? I thought, I'd really sooner this little tart than the woman I've married, I'd sooner spend my time with her, I'd sooner be able to use what I earn to cover everything, when I'm in the money I can do what I like and when I'm not there's no one to worry about except myself. I stood on the bridge over this canal, with all the lights shining or rather glowing, because they had these coloured bulbs, the girls, which were very strong but didn't throw any light, just glowed very intensely, and I waited as usual, thinking Christ what a waste of money and at the same time feeling my cock stiffening up and thinking there's nothing else in the world matters, nothing else I want to do but this, stand here, watch and then go in, but especially stand and watch, be at the moment before I went in, anticipation, you can't beat it I suppose. Well, there I stood, in the usual place, out of the line of men walking up and down the quay and at the same time in a good position to nip in ahead of anyone I wanted to save her from. After a bit, I saw a bloke coming, a fat man, could have been a senior steward, he had this self-important air and at the same time he had his eye open for anything he could nick on the quiet, and I thought she's not having that bastard having it off with her. He got to the cobbles at the bottom of the bridge and I thought now's the time, cut him off, only I didn't. I didn't move. He walked up to her window, stared in at her, and I was feeling so sick I could hardly look and then he walked on and I thought you cunt, think you can do better, do you? I was confused, I didn't know what I wanted to happen. I felt as if I was reeling, as if I might drop straight into the canal, only I didn't of course, I'd only had a couple of Bols and a couple of glasses of draught lager to wash them down, and then another bloke came along, not a seaman, a comfortable-looking bloke in a long black coat and a hat and carrying a briefcase, walking along as if he'd no idea this quarter existed, looking in at the windows as if they'd been stamp shops or something and I watched him and he went in at Brenda's door just like it was home, no hesitation, straight in the door. The curtains went across. I could see her put the bolt across like I was in there with them. I stood on the bridge and Christ she might have been my sister; I wasn't anything exactly, I wasn't indignant or excited, what I was more than anything was determined, riveted. Nothing could've budged me from that bridge. It wasn't that long, and the door opened and the bloke came out, looking just the same as when he went in, coat, hat, briefcase. He might've been selling her life insurance. I suppose funnier

78

things have happened. I waited to see how long it would be before she was ready for the next trick and then I couldn't wait any longer, I was running after this bloke along the quay. I was in such a hurry I nearly bumped into him and I thought God what if he turns round what will I say, but he didn't have any idea that I had any reason to be following him, naturally enough, and he didn't look round even, he wasn't bothered. I didn't know what I was going to do. He went right and headed back into the district, quite a severe-looking bloke, about forty-five, glasses, the kind of beak you don't like to come up in front of he might've been because he'd give you a lecture, and then he started looking in the windows of these shops they've got where you can buy F.L.'s in red white and blue if you want to, they've got them in these packets, fucking Union Jack outfits we used to call them, and books and these films, all that sort of business and I thought you bastard, aren't you ever satisfied, because he seemed like he was ready for something else, but he only hesitated for a bit and then he looked at his watch and he was off down towards the station. I followed him across the tram lines. It was dark and coming on to rain and the whole place was glistening. Trams moaning, the buses coming from all directions, it seemed miles across to the station. We got there finally and he checked the board and I wondered, because I couldn't be sure, where he was going and I actually wondered whether I shouldn't buy a ticket. I suppose I must have been affected by the alcohol or something because I found myself thinking now I had a perfect opportunity to kill somebody. I wasn't jealous or any of that business, I wasn't that worried about Brenda, it just jumped into my mind how if I knocked this geezer off no one would have any

79

reason to tie us up and yet we were tied up. It was like it was just between us, him and me, as if we had a private thing going between us that was no one else's business, like he was me and I was him. It was a filthy night, like the ones in the stories my mother used to read, those thrillers she used to lend me, these murders and meetings they always took place on filthy nights that seemed to last for ever, like the nights in the Newdike because you never went there in the day-time. I wouldn't rob him or anything, I'd just want him to know that I was going to get him, just see the look in his eye and then I'd chuck him out of the train or something like that and be back on board before anyone started checking up. And however hard they checked, they could never point the finger at me. I was a sort of invisible man in his life. I was God. I felt so cunning it's funny, as if I was carrying a case full of atomic secrets or the plans of the future, as if I'd got clean through the customs with the biggest load of contraband ever. My bloke looked at his watch again and then he was off to the buffet. It was quite crowded because these Dutchmen they're always pigging it every hour of the day and night, they like their grub all right, so I had one of those open sandwiches and I strolled along and then, as if by chance, I'm dropping into a seat at the same table. He's got a gold tooth that worries him, he keeps touching it with his tongue and his eyes get a funny faraway expression as if he'd got no further use for them and I'm thinking that's how he'll look when I get my fingers round his throat. Then he opens his briefcase and takes out some papers and changes his spectacles and he's working away, he could've been in his office or somewhere, making little marks in the margins and frowning at a word he doesn't like and I see him changing in front of my eyes so I have to keep reminding myself it's the same bloke I saw coming out of my little tart's hutch, out of Brenda's, and I can't believe he'd ever feel the need, it's as if I was losing touch with him, and at the same time I'm thinking that's right, you would, as if we were old mates, as if I knew him backwards, as if I was actually fond of him, sort of business. Meanwhile of course I'm sitting there and I feel a bit conspicuous, sipping this empty cup and pretending I'm killing time. He looks up at me eventually and keeps looking and I think Christ he's probably going to call a copper, he's probably decided it's gone beyond a joke and then he takes out his cigarette case, still looking at me, and opens it and suddenly he's smiling and then he says, 'Cigarette?' just like that, in English, as if he'd known all along exactly who I was. Woof, I felt queer. I said no thanks and I sat there for a bit, as if I was trying to remember something, and then I stood up and worked my way from behind the table and went out. I didn't know what to do. I didn't know whether to go back to the ship or what. I thought I'd have a beer, and when I came out of the station bar, I saw my character again standing with a crowd of people watching a train coming in and then I realized he'd come to the station to meet someone. So I stood around again. I was absolutely desperate only I don't know why. I felt as if I couldn't bear to be alone, as if by mistake, like taking the wrong coat when you leave a party or something, I'd got into the wrong body, as if I was a stranger to myself, like when you put your hands in the pockets of a coat and come out with someone else's keys, odd possessions you can't make complete sense of, a hand- kerchief, two torn cinema tickets and a receipt for some-

81

thing. It was a woman, of course, I suppose it was his wife, a dark woman, Spanish-looking, with two little kiss curls over her ears, black, doleful eyes and a fur coat, a little fat but not unattractive and he leads her back through the crowd and she's preening herself, it's her old man all right, and she's so pleased to be with him and so confident he's glad to see her you can tell she can't wait to get him back to the flat and get her knees up. I didn't think you bastard or anything like that; I just watched them go and I quite fancied her as a matter of fact. I went into the gents and I found myself thinking of her, this woman that'd come off the train and met this bloke, her husband I assume, and was walking along so proudly beside him when an hour before he'd been over Brenda in the Newdike. I didn't feel sorry for her or anything; on the contrary, I was excited thinking about her. She had very narrow red lips and sad, black eyes and she was plump under her fur coat you could tell, like a little pigeon. I wondered all sorts of things sitting there. If I'd had the time and the money I'd've followed them and found out where they lived and maybe taken a room so I could see their place, keep them under observation. I was excited by the idea of seeing them. I didn't care what they said; in fact hearing them talk to each other would spoil it really, hearing them chattering to each other in Dutch. I wondered if he did it for his sake or for hers, going to Brenda.

'She goes wrestling occasionally.'

Finally I went back to Lola. We'd found a room near her mother's where she could bring the baby. She talked about living with her old woman, but I wasn't risking anyone

82

checking up on what I said or where I went. So we found this room. It was at the top of a vicarage, with a side staircase up a tower, I don't know what it had been, anyway it was all right and there she was, waiting for me. She said, 'So you're back,' and I said, 'Of course I'm back, how've you been?' It had been ten weeks, the Gulf and back and then we'd had to hang around before we got paid off. 'Did you think I wouldn't come back then, did you?' 'I didn't think anything,' she said. 'Well cheer up, because here I am,' and I felt this terrible depression, guilt really, as if I'd done something I shouldn't have, which as it happened wasn't the case at all. I said, 'Have you missed me?' And she gave me this funny look and nodded and I thought right, this is it, and I had her down on the ground and she was fighting me, at first I couldn't believe it, but she was, she was fighting me, she wasn't having any and I was choked, I can tell you that, I was bloody furious inside, bloody mad I was. Ten weeks and she's acting like the Virgin Mary. 'What's the matter with you?' I said. 'Aren't you this girl I was supposed to have got married to? What's the matter with you?' I was furious. I pulled it out just like that and showed it to her, 'What do you expect me to do with this?' I said to her. 'Take it to the Labour Exchange and get unemployment benefit on it? You'd better wake your ideas up.' I felt trapped then all right; I thought I'd go out of my mind. That calmed her down, but I was so angry I just turned away and put meself away and stared out of the window. If the vicar'd been down there I would've pissed on him. Christ I thought, England. It was a miserable day, raining, grey, the streets all jammed with cars, some dreary little crisis on the box. I turned the box on and there was some politician

83

smiling like an undertaker who's buried the wrong bloke but it's all going to be all right, only it'll cost a bit more. I thought I'd like to walk straight out, my bag was right there by the door, I thought I'd walk straight out and go to Australia or somewhere. And do what? Get mixed up with some woman and have the same thing all over again. One time I was in a bar down by the docks and this bloke started buying me drinks, chatting me up and I thought first time anyone's ever made a set at me, I took him for a pouffe, well dressed bloke, ring on his finger, flashy but very intense, spoke in this very precise voice, and finally when it came to the point it turned out he was some kind of crook, and he was looking for a bloke to do the strongarm stuff on a raid some mates of his were planning and was I interested? I was dead shocked to tell the truth, and scared. I said no, I wasn't having anything to do with it. I was quite insulted, just as if he had been after a bit of the other, I told him no, definitely not. Well, I thought of that bloke when Lo gave me the brushoff, I thought why not, why not get involved in something big enough to put you in the chips for good, shit or bust why not, because I could see I was trapped, helpless, I could see myself landed for good and all, doomed to a landscape without hills and I thought I'd do anything for a chance at something big. In fact I don't believe I could've thumped a watchman or whatever it was they wanted done, although I was quite tough, I don't really think I could've done it in cold blood, I think I would've been too squeamish. Apart from anything else I don't fancy thumping a bloke in case I thump too hard. Well, I stood there staring out of the window and thinking I must be bloody mad to let a woman put a ball and chain on me and then I felt her arms round my waist and I stood as cold as a statue, thinking you do the bloody work, you see what you can do, and I was working this little muscle in my cheek, like they do in the pictures, and I thought am I acting or do I really feel as angry, as unforgiving, as cold as I'm trying to? I don't remember ever doing that muscle thing before and it seems almost like a division in my life, because I've done it ever since, when I'm choked, when I can't say anything.

'Aren't things a price? I don't know.'

I decided, I don't know why, while I was standing there, hating her guts, that Lo ought to have some money of her own. She put her arm round me and not wanting her, hating her, I said, 'You don't trust me.' She said, 'It's only the baby.' 'What do you mean only the baby? What is?' 'I might lose it. It's the Month, you know.' I didn't say anything for a moment. Then she said, 'Charlie ... ' And I said, 'Well at least you've remembered my name.' 'You shouldn't have married me.' I said, 'Why not? Not that you gave me a lot of choice.' I wanted her to cry. I didn't want to do anything else to her but I wanted her to cry. She said, 'I'm sorry.' I wasn't sure whether she was trying to cry or trying not to. Funny how you can't tell a thing from its opposite quite often. 'Forget it.' 'What can I do?' I said, 'Well, there's more ways of shelling peas than putting them through night school.' She said, 'More ways of what?' 'Forget it.' She did a funny thing then. I thought maybe she'd take the hint, I kept thinking of little Brenda and how you could wait for her to ask you what you wanted, I mean she'd give you the *à la carte* and you'd nod at whatever took your fancy, but you don't get that with a wife, not in my experience. What Lo did was, she took off her dress and put it across a chair and then she took off her underthings and her stockings, everything, and she was standing there naked on this ratty bit of carpet and I felt such hatred I couldn't move, couldn't turn, wouldn't. I stood there, I thought the sacrificial bloody lamb doesn't interest me, you can cross that off the menu thanks all the same. I could hear her coming up behind me and I swear she wasn't sobbing but I could hear the tears running down her cheeks. Of course I saw them really, like a very pale, shallow stream running over smooth pebbles, a steady stream there was, and still I thought you cunt, you've cut my balls off and you're only going to let me have them back when it suits you. I wasn't giving an inch. She was right by me and I glanced down, keeping the old muscle going, and I saw her feet. She had rather large pink feet, still has I suppose, and they were the most naked thing about her, because there they were on this ratty carpet, half on the fringe and half on the floor and I looked at them for a moment and then I was down on the lino under the window and kissing her feet. I was near crying, I was crying inside and kissing her feet, they were still warm from the shoes, and they smelt so clean and I looked up at her and her belly was just bowing a little, maybe it always would at that angle and there she was, all there was of her, and her hair hanging loose and she was looking down at me and her eyes were so tender I felt the biggest bastard alive and I still didn't know what to do and she was touching my hair and saying, 'I love you, Charlie' and then I was holding her round the middle with my face against her cunt and she said, 'Come on,' and I shook my head, I couldn't help it, and

86

she lifted me against her tits like a baby and there were two people in me, a sly kind of devil and someone who really wanted to love her, really appreciated her, how she felt; we were so close and so far apart, all at once. When we were in bed she kissed me and then she took me between her tits, I didn't want her to, but she did and I felt grateful and hating, all at the same time, because it seemed as if she was taking something from me, even if it was only my anger, she took me between her tits and she kept kissing me and I thought all the time how moving it was and how I hated this trap she'd caught me in. I didn't love her for it, it didn't make me think how much I loved her, only how sad it all was, how bloody sad and pathetic, I felt for her but I felt a thousand miles from her as well.

'You don't know me.'

'It's got something in it I can't place. What is it? Herbs or something?'

'There are herbs in it.'

'And something else is there?'

'Aren't you suspicious! You do sound suspicious!'

'I thought I was being appreciative.'

'I'm not poisoning you, if that's what you think.'

'Why should I think that? You don't have any reason to poison me do you?'

'I don't know, do I?'

'I hope you do.'

'I don't know what you do.'

'You want me to tell you my day? You'll be asleep before it's over, I'll promise you that.'

'What about your night?'

'I don't think that'd exactly get an X certificate either.'

'No need to sound so bitter about it.'

'I say you've cooked a smashing meal and you're trying to find something to be upset about. You need a doctor or somebody, that's what I think sometimes. You ought to see somebody.'

'It would be nice.'

'Something's worrying you. What?'

'Worrying me? I don't think anything's worrying me.'

'You seem worried to me. As if you weren't quite sure about something. Is it something I can help about?'

'You? Help? I don't think so. I'm not worried about anything.'

'As if someone was going to blame you for something. It's not what you're going to do that worries you. It's what you're going to say.'

'Say? Who to?'

'How should I know? You want to justify yourself. You act as though you were the one who was deciding things, but you seem—I don't know—apprehensive. You seem as though you're afraid you might have to report to somebody, justify yourself to somebody, and you're not sure how.'

'That's your opinion, isn't it? You're entitled to your opinion.'

What I did, after I left the merchant service, was I went to work for this electrical firm because I had some knowledge of electrics, only they took me on as a salesman. I knew what they had in mind, of course, from the interviewer who'd been a two and a half striper R.N. which gave us something in common, perhaps he was the reason they took me on, anyway they sent me to school that was what it came to, finishing school you might say. They said my accent wasn't precisely what they needed for salesmen; they didn't say it in so many words but that was the drift. They taught us a lot of phrases, sales technique, tricks for putting clients at their ease, all sorts of nonsense you never think about but which is important when it comes to selling. Now I was used to a fairly rough way of talking when I was at sea, I'd got used to it, it made you feel at one with the rest of the blokes honestly and I thought I'd find it difficult to get rid of, I thought it was part of the real me, but I found it wasn't so at all. I did use language a bit more than some of the other chaps on the course, people who'd come more or less direct from school and that kind of business, but I soon calmed down, I suppose you could call it, smoothed myself out. The chap who was in charge, I think he must've thought I was a model pupil, or maybe just that he was a master teacher, but anyway I was a bit of a star turn after a bit, he'd be getting me to demonstrate various approaches to these kids, all of whom had seemed so much smoother than I was a few weeks before. The fact was he didn't really teach me; I seemed to remember, I seemed to know exactly how to talk in a more educated tone, if you like to put it that way, even though I don't have the faintest idea where I remembered it from. The rough talk I thought was so natural, it was sort of pushed down, I didn't lose it, but it was as if I was two people, one a rough sailor, who was saying what a load of cobblers it all was, and the other this smooth character selling electrical equipment and whipping out the monogrammed cigarette case at the critical moment to clinch the sale. The sailor didn't really seem any more real than the salesman. I distrusted them both, they distrusted each other, the salesman was always smiling, made my jaw ache and the sailor, I got tired of his jeering and his bloody ignorance. It was the same with Lola, I kept wanting to be faithful to her right the way through, there was the kid, David, and we'd found this little terrace house, didn't have much of a lease on it because the whole district was scheduled for demolition, this row of Victorian houses, they were planning to pull it down for a flyover, I kept telling myself that I was happy but there was always this other voice telling me I'd fallen for the oldest con in the world and then I'd find myself hating her, for no reason I could tell her, hating her and wishing she was dead. I'd go into these moods, I wouldn't talk to her. I'd be polite, but I wouldn't talk. I'd say, 'Have it your way, whatever it is, have it your way.' And she'd say, 'I don't understand you,' and I thought no you don't and if you did you'd be scared out of your wits and that would make me feel so fond of her I'd go over and kiss her and then ten to one one of the kids would want something or gash its knee, 'Where's the Germolene?' and all that and I'd see her go all maternal and I hated them and I hated her and I wanted to get the hell out. She'd never have sex any time except at night, not once the kids were walking, not once David knew what was happening, as she put it. She was so bloody controlled, all I wanted was to get her going enough to do it and fuck them. It stopped having anything to do with pleasure as such or love or desire, of course. I don't mean I wanted it right in front of their eyes, but she wouldn't even if they were playing in the garden, even if they were up the road on a Saturday at a friend's and it used to make me so angry I wasn't interested later when she was actually willing. I'd pretend not to be and then when she believed me and turned over and went to sleep, I'd think what am I doing here, what's in it for me, I'm not even getting my bloody oats and I'd stare at her and she'd be lying there and Christ I'd think what am I supposed to do with it, clean chimneys?

'You've got a girl, haven't you? You've got a girl, I know you have.'
'Well, I know I haven't, so now what're you going to do?'

What decentralization is it's persuading people that they ought to move out of the inner London area basically, move their offices, their main operation and come out to, in the present instance, Westfleet. It stands to reason because with this overspill taking place all the time you've got an enormous amount of labour – skilled labour, clerical staff, part-time wives, all those sort of people – easily available and you've got offices that can be designed, tailormade, to suit your requirements, whereas in the inner London area you've got a lot of people crowded into unsuitable and costly premises. To me it's work worth doing, making people understand the advantages of new plant, local labour, I mean it must be worth it in terms of reduced strain alone, because you only have to look at these people crowding into London every morning to see it can't be healthy, it can't make sense. As I say sometimes, as the drinks arrive, because you have to time these things, what's the percentage in being a sardine with cancer? What amazes me is how much people resist it even when they can't give you a single argument *for* resisting it. I talk to managing directors and people, highups of one kind and another, educated people, and I show them the figures, because I try to be as objective as I can, and they'll agree with me right down the line, they won't even pretend there's a flaw in my argument and yet they'll say, 'It's very difficult,' or 'I'll need to think this over very carefully,' and you can see that they're dying to find a way out, even though it makes sense in every way, financially included, to up stakes. Why won't people do what they know they ought to do? The funny thing is, I see these people come out to Westfleet, when eventually they do, and they settle down, they have all this modern plant, they have landscaping, they have clean air to breathe, new houses, and I can't bring myself to join them. I mean, we could buy a nice little house in Westfleet, the same size as the one we've got in Brands Manor but with all the latest fitments, built to infinitely better specifications than Brands Manor, the problem is partly, of course, what would I do, because I'm selling the advantages of a place I couldn't so easily find a job in myself, not once it's really operating. Moses and me, there's no place for either of us in the promised land.

'Are you the lady of the house?'

I was sitting in the bar of the Plantagenet waiting for Tim Wicks, because he'd been working on some facts and figures for this photographic processing firm I was having a meeting with next morning and there was this couple sitting at the bar. The Plantagenet Hotel is one of a new chain that specializes in what they call business hotels. The plan is, you'll eventually be able to get secretaries and copying facilities and conference rooms, all available in the hotel. Westfleet is scheduled for a hundred thousand people when it's finished, so you've got this 180-bedroom hotel, which is a fair sized hotel, in the middle of the business district where half the shops aren't let yet and a lot of the factories aren't much more than a big picture in front of a whacking great hole in the ground. Meanwhile most of the rooms aren't in use yet but the bars and restaurants, which are much more luxurious than anything in the district, are already as busy as the West End practically. You've got all the Jags and Rovers in the car park, belonging to all these comfortable people from the stockbroker belt, they use the Plantagenet I think mostly for meeting each other's wives, because it's already got this atmosphere, which is strange in a place that wasn't in business eighteen months ago, this atmosphere of secrecy, as if it was full of dark corners. Anyway, I was in the bar, which has these cylindrical lights hanging on low wires from the ceiling right down over the shiny black tables, as well as a long bar with high stools, leather bucket type seats, and there was this couple, this man and this woman, she must have been about forty, he was a bit older and he was saying how bloody miserable he was, he'd had one or two and he'd got to the maudlin stage, and he was saying how life wasn't worth living and women were always after you, meaning wanting things out of you, not chasing you, at least that's what I gathered, and this woman she was twisting her legs round this steel shaft that held the seat up, and smiling in a funny way and staring at this onion because she was drinking what I discovered was a Gibson, because she said, 'A Gibson's the only drink I really like these days,' to the barman, she had the knack of talking to the barman as well as seeming to be alone with this bloke who was cursing his luck and saying he hadn't met a decent woman in years and he'd do anything to find one. I don't know whether he'd just picked this woman up, because she looked as if she wasn't above a bit of that, or whether they had drinks together all the time or whether it was his old woman even, you couldn't be sure. All he wanted really was someone to care for, he didn't want anything out of it, he just wanted someone he could be with, someone he could trust. 'And who could trust you?' she said to him all of a sudden, 'Have you thought about that? The way you behave?' 'How do I behave? What's so wrong about the way I behave?' 'I mean men,' she said, 'I'm sick of listening to them say how they only want to find someone to love, men want just one thing as you can very easily tell by seeing what happens when you won't give it to them.' 'I'm sorry, that's just not true. Assuming you're talking about sex.' 'I don't just mean beddybyes,' she said, 'I mean they want you to keep telling them how wonderful they are at it and they're so bloody awful most of them it makes you want to spit. I'm sick of holding men's heads while they bring up their past, sick and tired of it.' 'Then don't do it,' he said, 'and don't drink my drinks telling me how awful it is.' She threw her glass at him (good and empty) and it missed him, fell into this snowdrift carpet with a soft thud and lay there. 'Life could be so wonderful,' he said. 'Not with you it couldn't,' she said and she got down off this stool and I was fancying her like mad,

94

at the same time thinking why do you let her get away with it, the bitch? I fancied ramming her solid and throttling her at the same time. She walked out of the bar and left him sitting there and he didn't seem to know what had happened exactly. He sort of frowned, as if he'd been distracted, and ordered another.

'Sometimes I'm so frightened. I can't tell you how frightened.'
'Frightened of what?'
'Frightened. You don't know what it's like being alone.'
'It doesn't happen that often.'
'No, but when it does.'

'What was that?'
'What was what?'
'That.'

'There's only one thing that sort of person understands, one of them said, and then the other one said, I know, and the first one said, only one thing to do and that's put the frighteners on him. I heard them say that. That's the sort of thing—'
'That's nothing to get upset about. A crossed line's got nothing to do with you.'
'I called the police and they said they couldn't do anything. There was nothing they could do. I'm frightened, when I think of people like that in the world.'
'How many times do I have to tell you? Nobody's going to do anything to you.'

*

'Wife trouble, old man?'

When Tim Wicks finally turned up and asked me, 'What're you having?' I told him a Gibson and this bloke, he was still sitting at the bar, he looked at me like he could have killed me. What I wondered was, where had the woman gone? She had on this fur coat, of course, they always have those, trophies of war, but was she waiting for him outside or did she have her own car or what? I suppose she could have been somebody else's wife and had the second car outside (where does the money come from, that's what I'd like to know, the meals these people order, caviare, smoked salmon, grouse, where does it come from?) or she could have been staying, only I don't know what for. Funny the way a woman can walk out and not seem to think where she's going. I felt sorry for those two, when I thought about it later, when I was up in my room (I just got the box switched off before they played the Queen) and then I thought about Lo and I thought I'll call her and then I thought no I won't, I'll go and see her and then a sort of terrible thought came into my head, what if I went home and found her dead when I was going to tell her how much I loved her, wouldn't that be an authentic tragedy? And then I wondered could I get there and back without leaving a single clue that I'd gone. I never had in mind to do anything to her when it first came into my head, I was thinking how much better off I was than that poor benighted sod in the bar and how we had the kids and the house and things weren't so bad and then all these other ideas came crowding in and I wished they hadn't. Anyway, I got dressed and I thought this is bloody ridiculous because it was ten after twelve by this time and it was just under two hours to Brands Manor at the best of times and if I speeded and got nicked I'd run the risk of blowing the whole shoot. I was driving myself potty there were so many voices going on in my head but I had this very strong urge at least to see her, not to let her know I was there, just see her, because otherwise there'd only be questions about why couldn't I come more often. All the way in the car I was thinking you must be crazy, I felt I was floating, not really out of bed at all. My clothes didn't feel right, even though I'd put on exactly what I always put on, all my clothes exactly as if it was morning. I'd had a bath before going to bed and I think that was what did it; I felt naked under my clothes, as if a layer was missing between me and my things. I left the car down behind this bowling alley they've built and are probably going to have to junk because people just don't seem to take to bowling in this country, don't ask me why, and I walked up past the parade and it was like coming back from the dead, still dead, but coming back. I felt transparent, superman and weak as a cat all at once. It was ten past two already because there was this hold-up at one of the big junctions where they were doing some emergency repairs; bloody great machines working away in the darkness. I'd decided on the way I'd go back a different way because I reckon no one will notice an 1100 going one way at night but the same car coming back, especially where you've got men working on the road and there was also a police car, might not be such a good idea. There's a little sort of alley down behind the houses in our row, just wide enough for David to cycle along and nearly kill me one time (he had his head down watching the new speedo) so I dodged up there. It's got gates

97

off it into the bottoms of the gardens. The floor's all wadded with leaves so you don't make any noise. I thought of taking my shoes off, but what if you meet a copper or something and you're carrying your shoes? It's not very convincing to say it's so as not to wake up your old woman, is it, but that would've been true, because already, in the open air, I felt as if it was indoors, as if the whole place had walls around it. I sprang the gate (no problem) and there I was, trembling, in my own back garden. There's a little shed where I keep a few tools for odd jobs and I stood next to it and stared at the house. A light was on downstairs, Lola left one on somewhere because she was afraid someone might notice the car wasn't there and think the house was unoccupied. More than anything she dreaded someone doing something to her by mistake. I was getting cold by this time and I felt a bit stupid because now I'd arrived I really didn't know what to do. I had a key, I could get into the house all right if I wanted to give her a surprise, but I dreaded explanations more than anything, like for instance why I'd left the car down the road. Then I thought, what if the house caught fire, what if I was standing there and I saw flames coming out of the windows, what would I do? I had a tin of kerosene I kept for burning weeds off the path and the drive, well the bit of concrete up to the garage, and I had this idea of sloshing some of it about, it doesn't burn like petrol, it doesn't explode in the same way, and setting light to it and at the same time I was thinking if the place was really on fire I'd dash in and save the kids and Lo and then she'd believe that I really cared for her, if I rescued her and the kids. Next time she said, 'You don't love me,' I'd be able to sigh and she'd have to think, he risked his life for me so what am I saying? Though of course the fact remains you'd do the same thing for some-body you'd never met in your life, without thinking prob-ably, so where does that leave you? All the same, it's not true we haven't cared for each other, sometimes we've been in bed and she's done something and I've thought I'd like to die, right now, because I don't want anything beyond this moment. I think it's all wrong that people have to go on and on until they've exhausted everything, until they don't want each other any more, it seems all wrong to me. I think that's what I hate most, the feeling that we'd once wanted each other so much and then we'd be sitting by the fire and she'd be doing some sewing with her glasses down her nose or something, or her stockings all wrinkled, and I'd be watching some dreadful television show and I'd think Christ once upon a time she couldn't wait for it and I'd think of her all hot like she was that first time, and I'd think Christ she actually wants her mother over to see us now, she's actually asked the old cow over and I'd think of her heel out of her shoe when she was putting away those dishes and I'd want to strangle her. All those faces smiling at you out of the *TV Times* or whatever it was, I'd want to screw it up and chuck it at her. I hate those toothy smiles people put on in those photographs. What kind of fools do they think we are, all those television people? Everyone thinks you're a fool today. They keep you from the world, those smiling people, 'presenting' things to you you're really paying for, being each other's 'guests', doing you a favour letting you have what you're entitled to anyway. And the young people, everyone says they're wonderful or they're dreadful or whatever they say they are, well I don't care much about them one way or the other, except one thing I'm tired of hearing them talk about society, how society's done this or hasn't done that because quite frankly I don't find there's that much of it about, society, England's England and that's about it, the rest you do for yourself. They grumble all the time and I see them all together, out at night or whatever they're doing and they don't look to be having such a bad time quite frankly, they've got money and they can do what they please, as far as I can see, and we're supposed to feel we've let them down, I get that feeling already with David, with my son, how any minute he's going to be telling me how I've let him down and I think Christ you've got all yours to come, he's waiting for the day when he gets his first girl to take her things off and he can look at her and think Christ all mine, where do I begin, whereas me, I'm wondering where it's all gone, wondering if she's going to have curlers in, she's taken to those plastic curlers and it takes a bit of imagination to get randy with that lot staring you in the face. I try to talk to him sometimes, David. I say to him, do what you want only don't get caught and all he's thinking, ten to one, is no I won't, at least not by you, you bastard, I can see it in his eyes. He won't do a blind thing around the house, won't do a hand's turn and next thing he'll be telling me where I went wrong. I took out this tin of kerosene, I actually had the cap off and then I thought what's the matter with you, are you out of your mind? So I stood there sniffing the stuff and then I saw a movement in the house. I dodged behind the shed sharpish like a burglar, I thought what can I say, I was scared stiff, my heart was thumping like the big end had gone. The light shifted, that was all, maybe it was just a draught or something like that, blowing a door, because nothing more seemed to happen, and I was O.K. for a moment and then I thought maybe she's gone to telephone the police. I thought they'd maybe throw a cordon around the block and then what would I do? I began to think it was all a dream, that I might as well wake up now because nothing more was going to happen. I was very tired actually all of a sudden, because I couldn't see any future, except this miserable drive back I had in front of me. Then I thought I really would like to see her. I wondered was she really there, was she really at home all these nights I was away and I thought then, even more than ever before, I don't know her at all, I don't know her from Adam, Eve anyway. For years I couldn't bear hearing her in the lavatory, I thought if I hear her dropping a big one I won't ever fancy her again, I was superstitious about it, but I did one day and nothing seemed to change, my attitude didn't seem to change. Wanting people doesn't seem to have much to do with them, not really, that's what I've discovered. I crept down the path like I was playing grandmother's footsteps, stop start, stop start. While I was creeping down the path and up the side of the house, it suddenly came to me that she had some money. I'd given her some money, Lola, when we first got married and now and again I'd slip her a few quid if I'd had a good month, got a bit of commission, I never did it very nicely, I'll admit that, as if it was something she'd demanded, whereas, in fact, she's very good about money; it's not the money she begrudges me, it's the freedom, the freedom, that is, to go out to work, because that's what it comes to. I sometimes think if women had the same freedom men have they'd be having it off from morning to night because that seems to be what they assume you're doing when ten to one you're talking about comparative statistics or some such stimulating topic with a bloke who's happy to smoke yours and never dreams of offering you one of his. This money, I'd never want to be thanked for it. I'd react as if she was a hypocrite thanking me. I'd say 'forget it' and plonk it down as if I was behind on the payments for something and I'd not talk to her for quite a bit afterwards sometimes; it might have been blackmail. Suddenly that night I wondered what she's done with it and I couldn't imagine, and that made me realize again that I didn't really know her, not really. People are like these solid objects that aren't really solid at all, that have all this emptiness in them, all this empty space and we say we recognize them, see them whole and we don't at all, we just deliberately refuse to see the empty bits, we refuse to allow them not to be solid, to be as unreliable as we are ourselves. We recognize a bit here and another bit there and we join them up with a straight line and assume that's the real shape the person has, that's his character, because we want to rely on it; we really resent it if he turns out not to be like we've decided he is. It's like when you're driving, you go over the top of a hill, you assume the road goes on on the far side. The time you're wrong, you're dead most likely. She didn't keep it around the house as far as I knew. Did she have a bank or had she blown it on something I didn't know about? I thought, you cunning cow aren't you, what've you done with it? And there I was at the front door and trying to shove the key into it as silently as I could and then there was a click and I was in my own house and shaking. I was nearly shitting myself walking into my own house. I thought if she comes down and catches me it'll be the end, I shall have to kill her, because what else can I do?

'There isn't going to be any fuss, because if there is, you know what I'll do.'

I might never have been there before in my life. I might never have seen any of the stuff before, my own furniture. It was like one of these transformation scenes they used to have in pantomimes when I was a kid, and the whole place'd suddenly turn into an enchanted castle and there'd be mirrors everywhere and chandeliers, and search me how it got there. Of course there wasn't anything like that, it was my own house all right; no chandeliers, only our usual stuff in the usual places, no one'd been waving magic wands in my absence, no such luck, but it was strange all the same, I was shaking so I couldn't get my breath, like I was going to have a heart attack. I was scared because it was against all my plans, if she came down and I had to kill her like this, it'd be disastrous, it'd just be the burglar being rumbled and doing the householder, and that's not too clever. I padded about the place a bit and then I thought I'd do something, it sounds ridiculous, but I had a very strong urge to take a leak, nerves I suppose, and I thought if I use the W.C. it'll make a noise, she might hear something. I remember once I was with some woman in her hutch, some woman I'd picked up on a shore leave, in a pub, and we were up at her place, her old man was away, I can't have been much more than nineteen, and she was well away, obviously mad for it, only I didn't realize, I thought it was me, how clever I was being, getting her things open and that, I'd had a few drinks, I'd met her in this pub, and I had this terrific need for a slash, so I eased off, as if I was having scruples or something and then finally I said I wanted a drink of water and I went into her W.C. to take a

103

leak and I couldn't scarcely start because apart from anything else I thought Christ if she hears me and then I go back, it's going to ruin the atmosphere. I ran the tap and pretended to be washing my hands and washing the glass and that and then of course I went back and she knew very well what I'd been doing, didn't take much guessing, and she was lying there just as I left her, didn't give a damn, she just looked up and smiled and said, 'Better?' Talk about feeling a fool! We had this big rubber plant in a plastic pot by the front door, full of earth, it didn't make a sound, so I used that and then I got out as fast as I could. When I got back to the car I felt so bad I sat there shaking, I couldn't get the key in the starter, I felt so bad. I thought Christ anyone could do her, anyone could get into that house and do her and she wouldn't know what'd hit her; I felt terrible. Then it occurred to me she could've been lying upstairs in a pool of blood, she could've been lying there and I could've been her last chance and here I was charging off without so much as seeing her. After that I had to know if she was all right, so I started the car and when I'd gone a bit of the way back towards West-fleet I stopped at a kiosk and I dialled her number, our number. I thought if she's dead I'm going to devote the rest of my life to getting the bloke who's done her. It must have been quarter to three by this time, and I'm standing there waiting for the number to ring and what do I get? The engaged tone. I couldn't believe it, three o'clock in the morning and she's *engaged*, it's not possible, I couldn't believe it, who's she talking to at three o'clock in the morning? It had to be a wrong connection, so I tried again: engaged again. She was bloody well talking to someone at three o'clock in the morning. I thought should I wait, what should I do? I waited and it was still engaged. I called the operator, but she says the engineers aren't in, she gives me this long palaver and I'm so wrought up I can't talk to her, so I bang down the phone and go back to the car. It has to be a mistake, of course, because who talks on the phone at three in the morning? It's obviously a fault, obviously. Suddenly I realize I've got a meeting in a little less than five hours, so I get back in the car and drive back to the Plantagenet. I'm so flaked I don't even bother to take the alternative route. Just as well I didn't do anything to her. The switchboard girl was off at the hotel too, the one I was used to, and there was only this Irish night porter dozing by the keys and I thought skip it, I'll call her in the morning because if I didn't get some sleep I was never going to be able to impress these people. All the same, I lay there a good hour ticking like a time-bomb before I dropped off. In the morning it all seemed a bit different. I told myself it obviously was a fault in the line and if it wasn't how could I ever find out? Ask her who she was talking to at three in the morning? She'd think I was off my chump. All the same I felt something new, something I'd not felt before, I won't say I was suspicious, I didn't suspect her of anything exactly, I just thought, you never know, do you, she's supposed to be my wife and she could be doing anything.

'Lie down on the floor. Do as I say, you'd better.'

I had a good morning with these people, Croft and Deeping, it's quite a big outfit, I was surprised, and I don't think I ever talked better. What I told them must've made sense to them, apparently, because they were on to Lambert

Livingston that same afternoon. His secretary came into the office and told me, one of his secretaries, because he had two, three if you count the switchboard girl, she was quite new, Jean, and I always had the impression that she was too pleased with herself by half, she had this very educated voice and she seemed, I don't know how to describe it exactly, as if she was buttoned very tight into her clothes, she wore this pinafore dress with a belt round her middle and high heels and she had a fleshy look about her, but all very held in, not for the likes of you sort of thing. She wore spectacles and this orange lipstick, pale face and orange lipstick, Jean Haughton. I suppose that made me think she was a bit grand, haughty Haughton sort of thing. Anyway she came into where I was working, I don't have a secretary, I use a girl from the pool when I've got letters need doing, when I'm writing to people, and she said, 'Mr Livingston's very pleased with you,' and I said, 'I should think so,' and she gave me this little smile, as if she was the head girl and I'd done something right at last, and I wondered whether she was getting it regular and whether she was missing it if not. Miss Jean Haughton.

'What makes you think anything's going on?'

'Do you ever get phone calls when I'm away?'
'Phone calls? What do you mean?'
'People calling you on the phone? What else would I mean?'
'Do you mean does the phone ever ring when you're not here? Of course it does sometimes. Mother calls me. And I do have one or two friends—'

'I mean people you don't know. People ringing and then ringing off when you answer, that sort of thing, strange voices. In the middle of the night, for instance—'

'Why do you ask that? Why do you ask me that?'

'Why, do you?'

'Are you afraid someone'll call wanting to talk to you and I'll answer, is that it?'

'If I was afraid of that I'd hardly give them this number would I? I'd get them to call me at work or somewhere. I'm not that stupid.'

'I'm sure you've got it very carefully worked out.'

'I haven't got anything worked out. I was just wondering if these nerves of yours were anything to do with phone calls. Sometimes people do get these anonymous callers and they are, you know, very unpleasant.'

'Sometimes there's a wrong number, but not very often. Have you seen what's happened to my rubber plant?'

'Your rubber plant? What?'

'I don't know what's happened to it. It's lost all its spring.'

I smiled at her and she gave me this little secret smile, made me wonder which of us had a secret from the other. When I came into the bedroom that night she was lying under the bedclothes, I hardly gave her a look and then when I pulled them back to get in myself I saw she was naked, and when I looked at her, I was in my pyjamas myself, she gave me the same smile and I smiled back at her and we made love that night like we hadn't for years, she kept on being about to come, and I was holding her back, holding her back, we nearly drove each other crazy and I was thinking what else could I possibly want, what could I possibly have that'd be better than this, and at the same time, what's it all about?

'In what way does he seem different exactly?'

That weekend we went down to the seaside with David and Annabelle, took them down to the seaside, to Clacton, hordes of people, but it was something to do and when we parked the car, miles away from the pier, but the only place we could find, miles away, I got out and I was standing with my hand on the doorpost thing, looking at the sea and wondering what time we'd have to start back, and Lo was locking up from inside, making sure everything was shut, she was fanatical about that kind of thing, locking up, and suddenly she reaches across and grabs hold of my door, not realizing that my hand was still there and whack she slams it shut. I'm looking over the top of the car and I manage to snatch my fingers out somehow before the thing actually locks, but it's caught me right across the knuckles all the same and it's bloody agony, only she can't see my face because it's looking over the top of the car and anyway, of course, she doesn't have any idea of what she's done, all she does is give the door a good bang for luck and she's out of the car and off down the pavement after Annabelle to get her anorak on because sure as hell it's started spitting and David's already counting his money, dividing it up between sweets and dodgems and telling everyone to shut up he's counting. The knuckles don't bleed right away, they hurt like hell and then they begin to ooze because the skin's all puckered up and I'm standing there and Lo calls out 'Aren't you coming?' and I think to myself there's no difference really, is there, whether you've done something on purpose or not, there's no difference, and at the same time my hand doesn't seem to hurt any more and I look and it's dripping into the road. I hopped over the railing and went down and washed it in the sea and when I get back Lo's walking up and down and looking furious. 'Where've you been? What've you been doing?' Now I know very well that I only have to tell her what's happened and she'll be sympathetic right away, I know that perfectly well, but I can't do it. She looks so angry, so mean, I can't bring myself to say a word. 'What's the matter now?' she says and I think if she'd called me by my name I would've explained, but I just shake my head and I've got my handkerchief tight round my fingers and I think nothing's any use, nothing is any bloody use whatsoever. I tell you what I really resented, when I come to think about it, and that is the way after she'd shut the door on me, she couldn't lock it, couldn't get the little tit to go down, she opened it again and slammed it again and although I had my fingers out by that time I think it was that second slam hurt me most. It's amazing how one person can be right next to another and not know what they're suffering. The night I came home, the night we made love, the Friday, I felt as if I held her whole body, her whole soul, between my two hands, I felt as if I had complete possession of her, never mind what triggered it, the rubber plant or whatever it was, I felt I really had her and now she was standing there in that blue dress of hers I never much liked, not with her colouring, and these freckles all over her face and she seemed like a great lump of nothing very much thank you all the same. Nothing lasts, does it?

The Monday, I was in London, I was down in the East End seeing some people, as usual, it's non-stop this job, one moment they're thumping you on the back and the next

H   109

they're on to you what're you doing about this or that, and how come your expenses are up so much this week? Anyway I was down in the East End with these clothing people, there're still a lot of them down there and you wouldn't believe the conditions they work in, some of them. It makes me feel almost like a missionary, visiting these places and thinking of Westfleet and the fields and the clean premises they could be occupying. They weren't easy to talk to, these particular people, because they were always talking themselves, trying to persuade me that everything was fine the way it was, because they had their distribution organization right there convenient for the West End and they had this arrangement with a local haulier and how it'd taken years to build up a business like theirs and for why should they go to some place they'd never even heard of? I thought a bit of lunch might loosen them up but they wouldn't come because they had this special place they always went, gave them the grub they were used to, so I left them some literature and went out by myself. I felt so depressed for some reason, I thought I wouldn't bother going back to the office, not all the way out to Westfleet that afternoon, I'd call and see what was doing and tell them I was making a few visits and get off home. I kept wondering why I felt so low, I couldn't understand it. When I looked into myself there was nothing there, nothing happening, only the reflection of my own anxiety. I walked along, looking at restaurants, trying to decide where to go, I thought I'd have a sandwich and I waited in a queue and then I left before they served me because there was this man complaining about his omelette, he'd had an omelette, in the Waitress Service section, and they asked him five and six, he couldn't believe it, he kept saying it over and over 'Five and six?' and the Pakistani or whatever he was behind the counter, the manager, he said that was right, five and six, and the bloke said, 'Five and six without chips, without chips, five and six?' and it did seem a bit much, I must say, only he didn't half go on about it and he had this hat and briefcase and an accent, I thought he might have been a solicitor, as if he'd done this place a thumping great favour coming into it. He didn't half go on about it until in the end I thought they might as well have asked him ten bob and let him make a fuss about that, anyway I walked out and he was still complaining and later I saw him getting into his car still shaking his head and I thought if it's five and six, it's five and six, and shut up about it. I ended up with a curry. Funny about curry, I keep trying to tell myself I like it and I never do, I always leave half of it. I always say 'Won't be too hot, will it?' and they say no, it's not hot, and next thing you're sending for the fire brigade to put the bastard out. Whenever I see people in a film or on the telly being led out to be shot or hanged or something—because they love showing you that bit, don't they?—I always wonder why don't they run for it or scream or beg for mercy, instead of just going along with it, stumbling along, not even trying to make a run for it, and there I was not half a mile from East India Dock and I still had my Union card, I could've found a ship and been away, slipped out of the country and no one would've known any better, I always keep my papers in order, but did I budge? Did I fuck. I sat there drinking this cloudy water they brought me and thinking, just like the condemned man in the pictures, there's nothing I can do, I've had it. I called the office and there wasn't anything needed attending to so

I said I had this client, a long shot I said it was, and there I was, free the whole afternoon! I bought a paper, but I couldn't find anything I was interested in. A funny feeling came over me suddenly; I had the feeling that I was doing something I might be arrested for, I had the feeling that I was on dangerous ground. I was standing on the corner eating this apple I'd gone in and bought, one apple and they didn't half make me feel I was some kind of nut, buying one apple, it's amazing how keen people are in this country to make you feel you're doing something that isn't normally done, something they could clobber you for if they felt like it. Anyway, I had this feeling so strongly that someone was going to clap me on the shoulder and take me away and make me confess to something, that in the end I went back to the car and I drove about, but once you're in a car you don't feel like taking the trouble to stop again, not with parking the way it is, so I drove home, that was all I could think to do with my free afternoon, pathetic when you think about it. I admit I thought of a strip club, because they show you everything these days, these strip clubs, they show you the lot, but even so, even when they show you a naked woman, I mean hairs and everything, it leaves you feeling cheated, leaves you feeling she's keeping something back, she isn't really stripped at all, that's my experience. It was about four fifteen that was all and I thought well at least no one can accuse me of anything if I go straight home, so home I went, all smiles. I went in all smiles and would you believe it? There wasn't a soul there. I looked at my watch and I thought surely the children were out of school by now and where was everybody, then I heard laughing and I looked out of the window and I could hear laughter coming

112

from the bottom of the garden. It was David and some friend of his, down by the shed, I couldn't see them but I recognized David and obviously it was some friend he had with him and I couldn't help it, I got the idea they knew I was coming home and they were laughing at me, as if they were in on some secret I wasn't. I went into the sitting-room and started looking at the damned *Radio Times* and then, like you do, I turned on the telly all the same, because you always think maybe there'll be something better on than's printed in the paper. By the time I went down the garden to see if David knew anything about his mother there was no one there. I trailed back and watched some children's programme and then I went upstairs and started looking for the suicide note. I thought, 'Perhaps it's the afternoon of the tragedy,' Lo's gone and done something desperate and I'm sitting waiting to welcome her home while all the time she's slowly turning blue in a gas-filled room, unless of course she's done a bunk, left me a sandwich and a dearjohn on the mantelpiece in the bedroom and done a bunk. I couldn't really believe that, not really, but I dashed up into the attic to see if the suitcases were still there and they were, so if she'd walked out she'd walked out in what she stood up in, she hadn't taken anything with her. I had visions of the frogmen plunging into the canal and tracker dogs sniffing in the long grass and some cod-eyed bastard asking me how I felt on the box and why was I convinced she was still alive? I went through her wardrobe and I'd built her this fitted dressing shelf with a drawer in it and a mirror along the top so I had a hunt through that. Of course I didn't find anything, only the usual pots and stuff. I told myself it was a good chance to read a book but there wasn't anything in the house I wanted to read. I went into David's room but I couldn't find anything there either, I don't know where he hides his titmags, but I couldn't find any anywhere. I suppose he was out there with his mate goggling over some dolly with a staple in her navel. Twenty to six in comes Lo, with a string bag of groceries, only not exactly supplies for the month, she couldn't have taken two hours getting that lot, and when she sees me she doesn't seem surprised or anything. She just walks around, putting things away, taking things out for the kids' supper, acting as if I wasn't there hardly. Eventually I said, 'Where's Annabelle?' and she said, 'Out to tea, why?' 'Well naturally I wondered where she was.' 'She's gone out to tea with a friend.' 'You can't blame me for wondering. I've been here since four o'clock, just before in fact. I got off early.' All she does is turn on the oven. 'You might at least acknowledge my existence, I've been here since four o'clock.' She straightens up and she gives me a look, I don't know how to take it, almost as if she's sorry for me, and she's brushing the hair out of her eyes and then she turns and walks out of the kitchen. I felt like smashing something. I went upstairs and she's in the W.C., I shouted at her, 'What've I done? What'm I supposed to have done?' I feel like I've just been sentenced to death. Finally I said, 'You haven't been to the doctor's, have you?' because I thought perhaps she'd been to the doctor's and it was some kind of bad news, doomed wife's courageous silence sort of business. 'Are you all right? Because I want to know.' I thought what am I going to say to Annabelle when she gets back, how'm I going to explain her mother's decided to spend the rest of her life in the W.C? She wouldn't answer so finally I lost my temper, I shouted out, 'O.K., whatever it is I'm sorry, I only

114

came home to see you and I was disappointed you weren't here, that's all, I don't know what you're upset about.'

'Do you wish you could leave me sometimes?'

I said to her that night, 'Lo, I want to talk to you.'

She said, 'That makes a nice change. What about?'

'Seriously, do you think I ought to turn this job in? I think it's making you unhappy and if it is I'd sooner turn it in.'

'Have you been offered something else?'

'No, but I don't think that's too much of a problem. I've had offers in the past.'

'Don't do anything for my sake, that's all I ask.'

'I wish you'd tell me what I'm supposed to have done.'

'Did I say you'd done anything?'

'Look, let's not mess about, there's been an atmosphere in this house you could cut with a knife ever since you got home, I mean if you don't want to tell me, O.K., if it's just a mood, fine, only I'd like to be told, I'd like to know, I really would.'

'I don't think you would,' she said, 'not really.'

'If it's something I've done, I'd like to know what it is.'

'It's nothing you've done.'

'Then what the hell is it? Because I feel as if I've done something!'

'You don't want me to have a life, do you?'

'Not want you to have a life? What's that supposed to mean?'

'What it says.'

'I think you'd better explain, frankly, I think you better had.'

'You don't love me,' she said, 'so why do you want me?'

'All right, go. Go on. Go. Only you'd better come back.'

I said, 'I used to have one of those,' and she looked up and said, 'You can have this one as far as I'm concerned.' 'Trouble?' 'Is right. I can't get it to do anything. I can't get it to budge.' I said, 'What'll you give me if I fix it?' and she said, 'Anything you like,' and I said, 'Right,' and grinned at her because I knew exactly what it was, it was the starting engine jammed, it'd happened to me dozens of times when I had the same car, so it was up with the old bonnet and off with the cap and give the tit a little twist and then I said, 'Try it now,' and she did and nothing happened at all, which gave us a bit of a laugh, but that was just the first time because I gave it another turn and that did it and she started and that was it, she drove straight off, with a wave admittedly. Next day I saw her I said, 'You never stopped to find out what I liked,' and she smiled, that same little smile I'd always taken to be stuck up and she said, 'I think I know what you like,' and I thought hello it's my day for two lumps because I reckoned I could've had her down on the floor right there and then in Lambert Livingston's outer office. It was a funny thing though because she didn't appear any different, she didn't look any different, it was as if you were outside a house and thinking you'd never get in and suddenly you were in, looking through the same windows but from the inside. At that time I hadn't been with another woman since Lola. Unless you count once I went to a party with a bunch of people from another firm and I had a girl, one of their

116

typists I suppose she was, in the stationery stock room only I hardly count that because she didn't know who I was and I didn't know who she was and it didn't mean a thing except sometimes it occurs to me I could have a kid walking around somewhere and I'll never know if I have or not. Anyway when she came out after work I was waiting in the 1100 and I said, 'How about trying a reliable car for a change?' and she gave me this snotty look of hers and got into her car which was next to mine, at least mine was next to hers because I'd slipped it in there in the morning, and she slid right through her car and out the other side and I thought well tonight really is my guest night. We went to a pub I'd never been to before, down on the towpath somewhere, it was black and white and stood all by itself, with rooms if you ever wanted to stay there, only it didn't look like any-one ever did, and three or four bars, none of them very busy, the main one with quite a decent view of the river, what-ever it was. I asked her what she wanted and we both had Double Diamonds and she said, 'You're married, aren't you?' and I said, 'Yes, and you're not are you?' and of course she wasn't so I said, 'Well there we are then, we both of us ought to be ashamed of ourselves,' and we laughed and that was the end of that. Afterwards we went in the car and I drove down this lane, and there was a dark copse at the top of it, like a deserted building, spooky with owls and rooks and I stopped the car and we started kissing each other like mad, and I was undoing her clothes, it was like Beat The Clock we were in such a hurry, I don't know if you remem-ber that programme. She was young, twenty-four or five, and I'd forgotten what young flesh felt like, quite honestly, I'd forgotten how solid it was. She didn't say anything, we

117

were both working away, it was bloody crowded in that car, I can tell you that. I suppose it can be done in an 1100 with the doors shut, because I'm sure people do it, but we couldn't, so in the end I opened the door so there was somewhere for the legs to go and we did it like that across the front seat. Luckily it was quite deserted up there, I'd turned down off the road along a track, and we just trusted to luck no one would happen along, it was about nine o'clock and getting dark, it was September, and all you could hear was us panting and the noise of the rooks and the cars along the main road.

She said to me, 'Charlie, what's going on?' and I said, 'Going on? I don't know what you're talking about, nothing's going on,' and she said, 'You're being so nice to me,' and she had this clever smile on her face. It was true; I was being nice to her. When I started going with Jean I thought it's the end I shan't be able to pretend to Lo that I'm not having it away because it'll show, I even wondered, because I didn't have much experience, whether I'd be able to make it with both of them in quick succession. Lo and I aren't everynighters but we're not once a month and twice on Christmas Eve either, and I thought what if she expects it when Jean and I have been at it just before, I shall never make it, I thought I couldn't possibly keep it up, but it didn't work out like that at all. It wasn't a matter of pretending to Lo either, that's the funny thing, the first night when I came home after Jean and me had started, I was like a kid's won a scholarship and doesn't have anyone to tell, but even then I got to the house and I thought poor old Lo, sitting around Brands Manor all day, never sees anybody different, so I drove on down to the Masonic Hospital because there's visiting there in the evenings and I knew there'd be a barrow outside and I bought her a bunch of flowers and it wasn't flannel, I wasn't being a hypocrite, I really thought poor little cow, no one caring about her, so I bought her half a dozen chrysanths, set me back fifteen bob. I was a lot more careful about hours once Jeannie and I were a regular thing. I stayed away nights as little as I possibly could and then only when I had a copperbottomed excuse, a meeting I could prove went on so late it'd have been stupid to drive all the way home, I used to work it all out to prove to Lo that I wasn't cheating on her. I had an entirely new feeling towards her, of responsibility. I was more worried about Jeannie than about her, in the sense of not doing right by her, not giving myself. Having Jeannie helped me see Lo in a different light, I don't say that I understood her or that I could see through her or anything, because I couldn't, obviously, but I saw her position and I felt more able to help her cope with it. As soon as I was having it away with Jeannie, I really thought we had quite a happy marriage, Lo and I, I was really very pleased with it, which made me feel I was letting Jeannie down in consequence. I wasn't so bad tempered any more, I had a lot more time for David, for my son, though he never had much for me, funny kid, never wanted to play football or anything like that or help me with a bit of carpentry at the weekends, not him, I don't know what he and this mate of his were up to but whatever it was, it was a wholetime occupation, I suppose they were wanking themselves silly or something, I don't know, good luck to them, but it left no time for woodwork, that I can promise you.

*

'Am I seeing you tonight?'

Saturdays I got in the way of taking Lo out, leaving the kids, because they'd just as soon have the house to themselves, and we'd go and have a Chinese meal or a mixed grill. They'd opened one of these classy new steak houses on the Broadway. They operate them on a franchise basis, these places, the manager was telling me; all the equipment's standardized, which keeps the costs down. Set me back about four quid all the same, that particular evening. It was worth it though because of this peculiar sensation I got, sitting there opposite Lo under all this tasteful lighting they'd put in, that I was with someone I'd never met before. It sounds bad, I know, but having Jeannie made Lo's company a lot more interesting than it had been in the days when I could only wonder how to get shot of her. As soon as I was well in with Jeannie, you know what I mean, I stopped having bad feelings about Lo. I didn't exactly have anything new to say to Lo, I mean we didn't suddenly talk about Shakespeare or the ballet or any of that business, but I was very happy just to sit and look at her. They take a lot of trouble over the lighting in those places, and I sat and stared at her, all sort of warm and golden-looking, and thought what a strange thing it was when a complete stranger's prepared to come and sit at your table, sit with you, look into your eyes, a complete stranger, and make conversation with you. I sat there and held her hand and asked her if everything was all right and even when I thought of Jeannie, who occasionally flashed through my mind, it only made me smile even more fondly at Lo than before. On the way home she'd snuggle up in the car and with any luck she was still warm as fresh toast when we got to the door and then as long as the kids were in bed, which ten to one they weren't, of course, the mood'd last right on into bed and I could make love to her without a word said from the time I'd put the car away. If I timed it right – I sometimes read a magazine for a bit sitting in the garage – she'd be already practically in bed before I came up and that meant that we could get down to it without any bloody discussion about the cat or whether the Ascot was functioning O.K. There wasn't any conflict, any risk of confusion I mean, between Lo and Jeannie, in bed I mean, because although Lo liked it, if the circumstances were right, she wasn't one for experiments or anything like that. She didn't have ideas. The result was, frankly, that Jeannie provided the spice and Lo provided the sweet side, and between the two of them I had a very balanced diet, thank you very much. When I only had Lo, when I thought I was sentenced to her for life, well, it was like always going on holiday to the same place, because variety wasn't her line, while with Jeannie you never knew where you were, it was the Magical Mystery Tour every time, and that gave things that touch of variety which is what a man likes basically. As for instance, she came up with this idea of how to do it in the car without opening the doors (you want to keep the warmth in when it comes to the end of October, beginning of November), it meant getting her feet wedged up against the ceiling, proper old acrobatics. I said to her, 'Would you mind explaining to me, Miss Haughton, how there come to be footprints on the interior roof of your vehicle?' and she came right back, 'A girl has to get her exercise where she can, Inspector, these days,' and at the same time she put on this cold, deadpan look, as if she was quite sure the managing

director wouldn't be able to see you till at least Friday fort-
night and probably not then and by the way what was the
name again? However, as I say, Lo must have had this
funny intuition or whatever you like to call it, because, out
of a clear blue sky as far as I was concerned, not many
seconds after she'd been lying there murmuring, 'Charlie,
Charlie, Charlie,' as if I'd just given her exactly what she
wanted for her birthday, which to be perfectly honest I
truly think I had, she suddenly said, 'What's going on?'
Mind you, she said it quite gently so I didn't think 'Whoops
here we go,' I didn't hear the sound of the guillotine
whistling down or anything like that. On the contrary I had
plenty of time to smile kindly, thinking at the same time, of
course, 'Watch it, Charlie, because this is the beginning,
this is the cloud no bigger than a man's whatsit,' and I
touched her face and said, 'Going on?' And she said, 'Yes.
Why're you being so nice to me all of a sudden?' and I said,
'All of a sudden, I don't know that I like that.' Diabolical,
isn't it, how easy it is to take offence when you're guilty of
something? 'Here was I thinking I'd been being nice to you
for quite a bit now.' She lets that sink in, like a hot horseshoe
in a snowdrift, for a little while and then she comes out with,
'Do you know what I used to think, Charlie, quite honestly?'
'What did you used to think?' Ready? 'I used to think you
hated me sometimes.' 'Did you really?' 'Yes, and you wanted
to get rid of me. I used to think sometimes you wanted to
kill me, to tell you the truth.' 'Kill you?' 'Yes, I did.' 'You
want to see a doctor, Lo, you do.' 'That's what I used to
think at one time. Be honest, Charlie, there was a time,
wasn't there, when you were jolly fed up with me, when
you wouldn't have minded if I'd gone under a bus or if the

ground had opened up and swallowed me, wasn't there?' 'I don't know how you can think such things. You've got a funny imagination, I must say.' 'There was.' 'I don't think there was.' 'So why have you changed?'

'Do you think she suspects something?' 'No, I truly don't, because I don't give her any cause to. I'm sure she doesn't.' 'Because I wouldn't like there to be any trouble.' 'There won't be.' 'I wouldn't like anything to come out.' 'Look, girl, nothing's going to come out. Of course you know the biggest danger? That someone'll see us in the car or meeting outside, a bit of pure bad luck like that.' 'Well, what do you suggest?' Jeannie was ambitious, you see, she wasn't worried about getting married, but she reckoned she had a good chance of getting made Lambert Livingston's assistant, which meant she'd be assistant general secretary of this whole Westfleet project and she didn't want anything to come between her and her dream, basically. She was like a man in that respect, now I come to think of it, a bit on the side was one thing, but she wasn't interested in getting hooked. It was actually part of the game that round the office we were as cold to each other as we could be. 'That Miss Haughton doesn't much like you, Mr Hanson,' one of the juniors said to me one day. 'Think so?' 'I know so. You should hear the things she says about your reports sometimes. Downright illiterate she said you were one day.' 'Bloody cow!' 'She did.' That was going a bit far, I thought, so I said to Jeannie next time we were together, 'What do you mean telling people I'm illiterate?' 'Well, so you are sometimes, the things you write, and anyway it's all for the best because it puts people off the scent, doesn't it?' 'Puts me off altogether,'

I said. 'No, it doesn't,' she said, 'and don't pretend it does, because I can see.' She had this way of exciting me no matter what I wanted, even when I was trying to make a point, as on this instance, I found myself making a point of an entirely different kind. Which didn't alter the fact that I was a bit choked, her telling people that I was illiterate. The thing was, though, it came out in sex, I mean it made me that bit more cunning, vicious even I was going to say, though I don't think I was ever that, and I've got a feeling that was what she was after all the time. In other words, she knew very well that little Lily Thomas, which was the name of this junior, who I now realize probably fancied me herself, in fact I'm certain of it, because she used to come down with these things she'd typed out for me and she smelt like they'd given her fourteen coats of Chanel Number Five and an extra one for luck, Jeannie knew very well, as I say, that the word would get back to me and that made me pinch her tit just that little bit harder, for instance, which was, I presume, exactly what she was after. Perhaps she thought I was a bit slow, because you never know what a woman is thinking, do you, I mean you're wondering will she let you and she's probably thinking why the hell doesn't he? 'You wouldn't want anyone to suspect, after all, would you?' Jeannie said, 'So it's best they should think we're at daggers drawn, rather than the alternative.' 'I'm getting sick of doing it in the car,' I said, 'like we have been doing, aren't you honestly?' 'Got a better idea, sailor?' 'Yes as a matter of fact.' It so happened that I'd been in Lambert Livingston's office that day and I'd seen them bringing in the furniture for the suite he was moving into, his permanent quarters, you might say, big buttoned sofas, but in this soft leather, the colour of toffee, that didn't stick to your skin, and I had this yen right away to get Jeannie on one of them – they must have carted in half a dozen, because there was the waiting room and then there was the office and then there was the outer office – and I suppose I was just waiting for the opportunity to mention them. And then he had this deep pile carpet and low lighting, these lights on steel rods you can slide up and down, which made me think a bit, all the sort of gear you couldn't buy if you saved up for half a century for your own house, only here it was, compliments of the ratepayer, being shipped into old Lambert's office as if it was the most natural thing in the world. I don't blame him, I mean why not have the best? But on the other hand it seemed such a shame, it not being used except for the occasional comfort of some tripey messenger or some la-de-da with arse-itch and only eight hours or so out of twenty-four. Ridiculous. So it occurred to me what a place for Jeannie and me to have our sessions. There wasn't a soul there after five thirty at night, because the pressure wasn't on at this stage and Lambert did most of his evening work in easy reach of a dry Martini, which meant he preferred the bar of the Plantagenet to most places, as who wouldn't? It just so happened that Jeannie and I had other tastes. 'It's risky, Charlie.' 'I don't agree.' 'Of course it is.' 'I don't agree. Frankly I think it's a lot more risky swanning around in cars and pubs and places. I mean you never know who might see us and pass the word. We're dead lucky no one has so far.' I made it sound like we'd been performing in a goldfish bowl. 'What if he comes back?' 'He won't. And anyway we'd hear the car, or something, and why should he? He likes to get off home after he's had his intake. The odds are it's safer in the office than anywhere.

And if he does come, we can always spread some papers on the floor and be working late by the time he gets upstairs. He always takes the lift and you know how long that takes, particularly if we make a point of bringing it up to the top before we get down to it, if you know what I mean.' 'I admit it'd be a lot more comfortable.' 'And chances are, if he does come back, he'll be so impressed with our devotion to duty, we'll get promotions on the spot.' 'Or he might want to join in,' she said. I said, 'Don't be disgusting. You are disgusting sometimes.' She really was. 'Come on, he's only human.' 'Can you swear to that? Have you got any evidence for it?' 'Oh I rather like Mr Livingston.' 'Do you really?' 'Yes, I do. And I don't think we should say anything against him.' Which didn't stop her agreeing to my plan. Typical of a woman, she goes off in a huff and comes back next time with everything worked out. She had the keys, she knew what the security arrangements were—nothing very elaborate in the event, since there were no valuables or anything like that, the confidential files were all locked up, so there wasn't really anything much anyone could want, which was a blessing—and it was all fixed. What we did was Jeannie established a routine, as they say, of working late. I think that was what first got her set on the idea, she realized that we could have it off that much more comfortably and at the same time she could get a reputation for extra effort, because she got permission, quite openly, you have to admire the girl, to stay on late because of some statistical survey she wanted to complete and all the papers were at the office and there was too many of them to take them home, and that meant, of course, that no one asked any questions if they saw a light on later than it ought to be, or anything like that. On the contrary, it'd be all the more credit to her, crafty cow. She cleared it with Lambert Livingston himself. Our plan was I left work as usual, if I was in the office, because quite often, as you'll appreciate, I was off seeing people, and then when the coast was clear, I'd drift back. I can tell you, I properly got the jumps the first time. I had to have a couple of pints and a short or two to steady me up. Then I wondered whether it was safe to take the car, because all I needed was to get nicked on the old breathalyser on the way back and have to go down to the station and God knows what. Jeannie wasn't the kind that'd take kindly to being let down when she was expecting her greens. I was that jittery I got the idea I was being watched, I got the idea someone had their eye on me, like when I was a kid and I used to lock myself in the bog before I dared to enjoy myself, that was what a friend of mine used to call it, in case someone saw me through a crack in the door or through the skylight or whatever it was. It's hard to get used to the idea that sex isn't something you have to hide. Anyway, I was that jumpy on the way back to the office, I parked the car and walked most of the way, although that was absolutely ridiculous logically, because nothing could have been more suspicious in the event there actually was someone watching. Then I wondered if she'd really be there. I couldn't believe my luck, because this was a sort of progression in my mind, getting her somewhere where we could operate more freely and I suppose it was a sort of a dream, a fantasy if you like, taking over Lambert Livingston's own suite. When the cat's away kind of business. The Development Corporation Offices are part of the whole general scheme, and so of course they're sited where it'll be most convenient when they've completed the whole shebang. In other words, they're bloody inconvenient at the moment, because they're slap in the middle of a damned great battlefield, frankly, it's the only way to describe it. There's only this narrow approach road through a mass of excavations, it looks like they're planning to bury the whole human race in a communal grave. Not much light either, although the standards are in, because they don't light them, all the light you get comes from the safety lanterns which make the place look even more spooky than before. The offices themselves are very well designed, I have to give them that, they're very handsome, to tell you the truth. And Lambert's got the pick, naturally, he's perched way up at the top, the penthouse effect, and when there's anything to survey apart from holes and billboards he'll be the monarch of it, assuming he lasts that long. Well, it looked dark when I first walked up, I wondered had she chickened out, though I didn't really think so, because she's not the type, only I thought perhaps something had gone wrong, but the key was where we'd planned it, on the ledge under the foundation stone that told you some drippy Minister'd done a day's work with a trowel laying it, and doubtless got taken off to get pissed afterwards for his pains. And they tell us to work harder. I opened the door, locked it behind me and went into the gents to have a quick slash, because as I say I'd had at least a couple of pints. They say if you keep a full bladder you go on longer with a woman, but it's not my experience, and anyway I think it's a bit indelicate, to tell you the truth, to rush off for a piss the moment you're finished. Christ, I stood there, I think that was the high point, standing there and thinking how really I had the best of both worlds. I looked down at myself and I thought what a perfect size I was. Sometimes you shrivel away to nothing and you wonder whether you'll ever come up to scratch again, you know what I mean, you look so scraggy. I'm thinking of when you've had an operation or even a bit of a temperature, though I sometimes find that illness can have an unexpected effect. I just seemed operationally perfect, although I was in the at ease position obviously enough. I had that nice fattened look about me, polite but ready to be at your service. Onward Christian Soldiers. The lift was at the top but I pressed the button and brought it down because I thought why should I walk for one thing and for another I wanted to check how much warning we'd have in the event of an emergency. You can't gauge these things during the day, because a building full of people is a different thing entirely. Anyway up she went and I stood there wondering where Jeannie'd be and what she'd be doing. You won't believe it, Lambert had one of these high-backed leather chairs, the kind that tilt and swivel and probably play God Save The Queen if you know where the button is and Jeannie was sitting in it, stark naked, leaning back and smoking a cigar. So how do you like that?

'I can't promise anything, you must understand that. I can't make any definite promises.'

It's a funny thing, you think of 'sleeping with someone', that particular expression I mean, as a way out of talking about what really happens. You know what I mean. You don't think of it as a proper description because when people talk about sleeping with someone, you don't think of shut-eye exactly. On the other hand, it occurred to me, reverting to Lo, that I really did sleep with her and I never had with Jeannie and that was the difference. For instance, I woke up one morning and there was Lo looking at me, standing by the side of the bed in her nightgown and looking at me. And the next morning, as if I was doing it on purpose, although I'm not one to wake early in the normal course, I woke up and lay there looking at her while she went on sleeping and I felt that soppy about her – I can't think of another way to express it – I could have cried. With that she looked up and her first smile of the morning, it seemed to crack her lips and she ran her tongue over them, and her face was pale pink, glowing, with the freckles all over it, like one of those globes they give to kids, with a light in the middle, it was as if a light had gone on inside her skull. She put her arms up and round me and she smelt fresh baked, like she'd just come out of the oven, she put her arms round me and she said, 'You know something, Charlie,' and I was wondering if we made love, because there was still at least ten minutes before the alarm, I was wondering if it'd put me off my stroke for the evening shift, because you have to think about things like that, seeing as I'd already fixed to see Jeannie, 'You know something,' Lo said, 'once upon a time I wouldn't have minded if you'd gone and left me, gone off and found yourself someone else, do you know that?' 'I'm glad you didn't tell me at the time,' I said, 'or I might've.' 'Only now,' she said, 'I'd kill you. You just try,' she said, 'because I'd kill you if you did.' 'Then why tell me to try it?' 'Because I couldn't bear it,' she said. And she's staring at me now, raised up on her elbow, as if I was a boy come late to school and she wasn't sure if my excuse was true or not. 'So don't you try it.' 'Catch me,' I said, 'when I'm perfectly happy as I am.' I had to be a bit cold-blooded about the nights I was going to be away, for one thing because Jeannie rather enjoyed teeing things up, she liked laying false trails and so forth, so that it seemed absolutely natural she should stay late and she didn't like being let down once we'd agreed in principle. She got so she even arranged it Lambert Livingston should ask her, as a particular favour, to have something ready next morning that would necessitate her working late. She loved to come out on top. The other thing was that Lo started taking a real interest in cookery. She prepared some fantastic meals and, of course, she was correspondingly displeased if I rang up suddenly and said I wasn't coming home. So in order not to upset her I had to make plans to deceive her well in advance, for her sake. I'd warn her of a conference coming up later in the week, say, which might mean I'd have to be at Westfleet early the next morning, in which case it probably wouldn't make sense for me to come all the way home, would it? And then the might would change into will and probably would change into certainly and I'd mention the traffic and the statistics of early morning accidents and finally I'd be free for Jeannie as per arrangement. Of course it didn't mean that I was able to spend the whole night with her even then, even if she'd wanted or been able to. She had her parents to keep sweet and I had the Plantagenet Hotel to think about, because if I wasn't there when they locked up and some idiot checked with the police and they called Lo there might be unfortunate consequences, to say the least. Everything had to be properly worked out, but I can't say I minded. Life had its rewards. One night for instance Lo did something absolutely fantastic, something she'd never done before and that was this meringue she did with ice cream in the centre. 'What's this then?' I asked her. 'It's called *Bombe Surprise*,' she said. 'Never heard of it. What's it all about then, got a bomb in the middle of it, has it?' She smiled at me and all she said was, 'You never know, do you?' It tasted all right though, I must say.

'You know I told you about this conference that's been threatening. I said I'd call you as soon as I could. Well, it seems it's on after all. Don't think I'm pleased, because it means I'm going to be at it till God knows what hour tonight. Unfortunately I have to earn a living. Only, I'll be home tomorrow night for certain. I might even get off a bit early if I'm lucky, tea time, because I've got a call to make round our way, so I'll try. If you're going to be there.'

'I'm a dull bastard actually, as you'd soon discover if you knew me better.' Funny saying that to a woman who's been half chewing your cock off a few minutes before, but there we were and she was lying back in the corner of the big sofa in the outer office with her mouth half open, lips all bruised and puffy and she was saying, almost to herself, 'You know, I don't really know the first thing about you.' Mind you, the first thing she certainly did know, frankly, if you take the same view of priorities as I do, but there was such a dreamy tone to her voice, I didn't like to intrude a vulgar note, not at that point. But a moment later, as soon as I'd said what I did, she'd completely changed. 'Oh I know that,' she said. 'I know you're a dull bastard,' and she winked and slowly swizzled herself round on the sofa and took the little mirror out of her bag and took a gander at herself. 'I

wasn't referring to your knowledge of the Peninsular War—'
'Whatever that may be.' 'I meant even in that department
where I fancy I know you quite well.' I was standing there
completely naked, which was a bit queer really, only I didn't
like to put my things back on too quickly. I mean rushing
into my clothes, it might look unsociable. It can take a bit of
time to get a woman to take her clothes off, but once they're
off you sometimes wonder if she's ever going to put them
back on again. What I usually did was to let her call the
tune. If she started getting into her gear, well then I'd follow
suit, but I believe in being tactful, especially when you've got
a girl like Jeannie who was quite capable of being very sarcastic. She'd already called me illiterate, after all. 'What
were you talking about exactly then?' 'Sex.' 'What else?'
'And what you'd really like to get up to. I mean, for instance,
do you ever want to kill me?' 'The goose that lays the golden
eggs? Not likely.' She said, 'There must be something. I
don't necessarily mean I want you to do it, but I wish I knew
what it was.' She sat there on the brown sofa, with her legs
crossed, as if she was interviewing me for a vacancy. Point
taken. She leaned sideways and took a cigarette out of her
bag and lit up, cool as you like, just as she was, the gas
lighter glinting on her specs, and took a deep breath. I like to
keep fit myself, so I don't really like to see anyone smoking
but it was a funny thing, the way she puffed up her chest,
and then sank back and smiled, it made me want to do it
too. 'I'll bet there are all sorts of things, only you haven't
got the guts to tell me.' 'I prefer doing to talking,' I said.
'All right,' she said. 'Only give it a bit,' I said, 'if you don't
mind.' 'It's a funny thing,' she said, 'we're only here so long
and you might say you couldn't be much closer to a man

than we've been to each other, one way and another, and yet there's tons we hide from each other, isn't there, as if we were sitting in a railway compartment and not exchanging a word?' 'You've done some funny things in railway compartments, then.' 'You're dead scared of being serious really, aren't you? You hide yourself all the time.' And there I am, naked as the day I was born, with my feet half hidden in Axminster at roughly four pound a square yard and nothing else hidden whatsoever. 'You'll never admit what you really fancy doing to me.' 'And what about you?' I said. 'If it comes to that.' 'I'm different,' she said, 'because part of what a woman wants is to have a man do what he wants, turn her into what he wants her to be.' 'And doesn't a man want the same thing?' 'That's what I want to know.' 'We all want to be used as well as doing things. Have things done to us. We don't necessarily know ourselves well enough, do we, to know what we really want, even if we're given the chance?' 'You're not quite such a stupid sod as I thought,' she said, 'not quite.' 'Thanks a lot, I must say.' 'You know,' she said, 'one of the things I've always wondered about?' 'What's that?' She comes over, still with a cigarette in her lips, it's funny really, and she takes my hand and then she goes and opens the door to the inner office, Lambert L.'s *sanctum sanctorum*, and she goes over to the window and pulls on the little plastic sticks which pull the cords and draws the curtains across, as if the show was about to begin. Then she presses on the shaded desk light, a half globe upside down which spills light right across the empty green hand-tooled leather and puddles in the big empty desk chair. 'Did you ever see that film where they were supposed to make love in a swivel chair?' 'Sounds kinky,' I said. 'No, I can't say I did.' 'The girl was sitting in the chair and the bloke came over and they were supposed to make it in the chair, it was more or less like this one, and the point is I don't believe it can be done.' 'Well,' I said, 'it depends which way up she finished, doesn't it, frankly?' 'You could see her legs, she was virtually sitting in the chair.' 'Maybe he came through the back,' I said, 'or drilled a hole in the bottom.' 'Or had a double jointed backbone.' 'Or a double jointed something else.' 'I don't think that would have helped. Look, how about like this?' 'Very nice of you to suggest it,' I said, 'but it's beyond me.' 'Literally.' 'Literally.' And we grinned at each other and then she was sitting there and her eyes were sharp and on a different tack entirely. 'What was that?' 'What was what?' 'That.' I went over to the window and looked out. There was no car in the car park I could see, but we were on the side. In my mind I was already racing to get my things back on. Jeannie didn't seem worried about that department. She opened the door and went into the next room. I followed her, so as to get near my clothes, because apart from anything else I didn't want a scene with Lambert Livingston to take place with me stark naked. I said, 'For God's sake tell me what—' 'Ssssh.' She opened the door into the passage and I couldn't hear anything, I was just going to say forget it when there was a sort of soft 'chonk' noise, I couldn't place it for a second, and then I realized, it was the fire door on the landing. 'Come on,' I said, 'for Christ's sake,' and I was getting into my clobber, because who wants to be caught with his pants literally down? 'Lambert!' she says. 'You don't have to tell me,' I said. 'Get dressed.' 'He said he was going home.' 'Never mind that, get your things on, you fucking woman.'

135

'Keep calm,' she said, 'I can cope.' 'You'll have to.' 'Don't worry.' 'What I don't understand though, is, why's he coming up the *stairs*?' I actually asked her that, while I was fiddling with my zip. 'What's it matter?' She was into her top and skirt like she was in the Olympics, I've never seen anyone do it so quickly, and we were down on the ground, spreading out papers like we wanted to have a picnic before the storm came. The door swung open just as I noticed that she hadn't put anything on under her sweater, and, believe it or not, despite expecting to hear old Lambert Livingston ask us what the hell we were at within a space of seconds, I was randy as hell at the sight of her tits through the wool, even though she'd been naked as you like a few minutes earlier and all I was hoping was that she wouldn't want it too soon because I wasn't really in the mood. Which proves, of course, there's more to sex than stripping off. As I say, we've both got our heads well down, as if all we were interested in was the good of the firm, and the door swings open and I'm waiting to hear the first cuckoo of spring when a voice says, 'Well, well,' and we both of us look up and whoever it is, it's not Lambert Livingston.

In case of emergency, break glass.

He's quite small and he's wearing a mackintosh and a flat cap. As I look up, he's trying to get something out of his pocket. I'll tell you the truth as it occurred to me, it looked as though he'd got a hard on, you know how it makes a big bulge in your pants, only his was in the wrong place, as if his cock grew out of his hip or somewhere, and before I can collect myself he's managed to get it out and of course it's this gun. I can see that moment over and over again, like you can a scoring chance when you're playing soccer and you twist and somehow you're all wrong to the ball and you see it go past, like a snail, an express snail, well that was the way it was with this bloke, because the moment the gun came up I know what I should've done. I could have collared him if I'd known what to expect going in, but I was expecting the boss and you can't dive at your boss's feet the moment he comes in the door, can you, in case he's going to pull a gun on you? Well, I've never seen such a change as came over this chap's face between when he couldn't get this thing out of his pocket and the moment it was safely lodged in his fist. I said, 'What's the bloody idea?' recovering as quickly as I could, which was nothing like quickly enough, of course, and he was breathing like he'd just run the Marathon. 'What're you doing here? Don't you know this is private property?' This little smirk comes across his face and he wags the gun. Even then I could hardly believe it, couldn't take it seriously, but it was a gun all right. Jeannie was still sorting out these papers on the floor as if she hadn't twigged yet, or as if the lights had come on while she was still setting the next scene and she didn't realize she was plumb in the middle of the action. Just then I saw her bra thing at the foot of the sofa and you won't believe this, even though this man was a burglar and it was none of his business I was more worried about pushing it out of sight than about the fact the idiot had a gun. I sort of hauled myself round so as to be between him and it and then started scooting backwards to get to it and push it out of sight. 'Just keep still, will you?' He was so nervous, this character, he could hardly raise his voice above a whisper.

He was that out of breath, I thought, Hullo, he's on the run, he's done somebody in or something and he's on the run and all he was hoping for was somewhere quiet to spend the night and now look what's happened. I had this feeling he was in a panic. He stepped round us as if we were nitro-glycerine and went over to the window and looked out. I had a sudden vision there was a whole lot more of them waiting outside, all in blue macs and greasy caps and all with guns that were too big for their pockets, but he came back and stood over us, because we were still down on the floor, only luckily in the meanwhile I'd managed to wedge Jeannie's bra under the sofa and I felt a lot better as a result. Jeannie finished piling up the papers and then she looked at me and raised her eyebrows, as much as to say, 'What've we got here then?' and all I could think to say was, 'Well, what have you been up to then?' He smiled, as if he was grateful for the opportunity, then he kind of cancelled the smile and said, 'I'll ask the questions.' And Jeannie looked sideways at me and bulged her eyes and I almost had to laugh. I should have crunched the little sod as he was struggling to get this thing out of course, but I hadn't and now, I have to admit it, I was almost glad, because he seemed such a pathetic little sod, it would've been a bit of an anticlimax to have landed him one before he could even get started and then called the coppers. And for obvious reasons I was quite glad not to have to call them, because you can imagine if we had. They'd start taking names and addresses and the next thing you know it's in the papers and Lo's not a fool, she'd be asking as many questions as the beak *and* passing judgment. It's ridiculous, I know, to dream of getting rid of someone and then to be so scared of giving them the chance to get rid of you, but that's the way it goes. Anyway, maybe I was a fool not to crunch him, as I say, but it was a bit of a novelty being held up by a bloke with a gun and it wasn't as though we had anything particular we wanted to do. I still had the feeling that when I had to settle him, I'd be able to without too much trouble, and meanwhile we'd just have some sport. Which is where I was wrong, of course. 'I was only thinking—' 'I said I'll ask the questions.' 'I wasn't going to ask a question.' Jeannie made a noise in her throat. 'You'd better shut up,' he said, and there was a really nasty note in his voice, as if she'd said something really sarcastic, as she sometimes can, and really stung him, although she hadn't actually done so in this instance. 'Look,' I said, 'we don't wish you any harm and frankly we were hoping not to be disturbed—' 'That I can well imagine.' 'Because we had some work to do.' 'Expect me to believe that?' 'I hardly see that it matters what you believe.' 'That's what you think. What were you doing just before?' 'Just before what?' 'Just before I came in.' 'I was sorting out these papers,' Jeannie said. 'You'll speak when you're spoken to and not otherwise.' 'Fine, I'll look forward to it.' 'When you're spoken to by me,' he said, as if he was closing some legal loophole. 'I want the true answer. About what you were doing.' 'I'll be perfectly honest,' I said, 'I don't really see what business it is of yours.' 'Well,' he said, 'you'll be surprised to hear that that's exactly what it is, my business.' 'We were having a chat, if you must know,' I said, 'while we were finishing what we were doing.' 'And what was that?' 'Sorting out—' 'I told you to shut up, I'm not telling you again. I'm talking to him, not you.' 'Sorry, it must be the way you're wearing your hat.' 'Look—' and he came right up to Jeannie and he was panting and I said,

'Look, steady on –' not sure exactly who I was talking to, him principally, but her too, like I was the referee and didn't want the game to turn nasty after only a few minutes of the first half. 'We were fucking if you really want to know,' Jeannie said. 'You were, were you? You dirty little scrubber, aren't you, eh? A dirty scrubber? I know your sort. Don't think I don't because I do.' Jeannie said, 'I wish you'd stop waggling that thing at us, because we're not going to do anything to you.' 'Does it occur to you I might do some- thing to you, does it? Because I should advise you to watch it.' 'All right,' she said, 'but it's not very –' 'Look,' and he stamped his foot, only it didn't make a sound because it was a first-grade Axminster and you can't make any impression on pile of that quality by stamping your foot. He'd polished his shoes, you could see that, but they were a cracked old pair, except for the toecaps, which were reasonably shiny. One of the little metal rings where the lace goes through had come adrift and was halfway across his instep, the right one, as I recall. 'What is it exactly that you're after?' I asked him, as if I had no personal axe to grind and just wanted to see everybody happy, if it could be managed, 'is it money?' 'Your sort of woman,' he said to Jeannie, he'd been staring at her all the while and never budged when I spoke, never took his eyes off her, 'you know what ought to happen to you. You ought to be stoned.' 'I'm sorry?' 'Stoned, I said.' My stomach turned over because I realized, Christ a nut! I mean: stoned! 'You mean stoned as in drugged or – ?' I wished she'd shut up at that point because if we were dealing with a nut, as we obviously were, there was no sense in being clever for clever's sake. 'I mean stoned as in the Old Testament,' he said. 'Because you know what you

140

are, don't you? You're the Whore of Babylon.' 'Oh of *course*,' she said, 'now you remind me—' He stared at her, and it was like a policeman, cold. 'Jeannie, don't—' I said. 'And you're no better,' he said. We were down on the ground still, like children who don't dare to get up. 'A married man. You are a married man, aren't you?' 'What's it got to do with you?' 'A married man carrying on with another woman and you don't see what it's got to do with me?' 'It's got nothing whatever to do with you.' 'You're going to get more than you bargained for, Miss, if you don't watch out.' I wasn't sure whether perhaps she had some plan, whether she had in mind to provoke him or distract him and wanted me to do something at some particular moment; I assumed so, because otherwise from what I could see she was just provoking him needlessly. I wasn't sure what attitude to take, whether to ignore her or pay her particular attention. It was like when you're next to someone in a traffic jam and they make faces at your back tyre, you don't know if they're trying to take the piss or whether the next time you accelerate your whole rear end's going to fall off. I said, 'I wish you'd tell us what you're after.' He just smiled at that, he seemed quite pleased, I felt like a prize pupil, you know what I mean, because he smiled at both of us, like now we were getting somewhere and he wouldn't have to keep us in after all. I said, 'How do you come to be here? Are you local or what?' 'Wouldn't you like to know?' Jeannie gave me a look that said, 'Hopeless case,' and she closed her eyes, as if she hoped when she opened them again it'd be her station and she could say goodnight because this was ridiculous. He said, 'It's got to stop, you know. It's got to stop, because if it doesn't—' 'What has?' I asked him, very politely, because I thought he might say fluoride in the water or battery hens, because there's no knowing what gets people steamed up these days. It might have been traffic wardens, or blacks, anything. He said, 'You know what I'm talking about. And don't you shut your eyes. Open your eyes and keep them open if you know what's good for you.' I said, 'Look, if it's money—' 'A lot of the trouble in the world's caused by people like you.' 'Is it? Do you really think that?' 'People carrying on like you two was carrying on.' Jeannie said, 'Was we carrying on, George?' She never could stand bad grammar, as I'd discovered for myself. I had to laugh though and that didn't please our friend. 'His name's not George and don't you pretend it is.' 'Isn't your name George? You haven't been deceiving me, have you? You haven't been lying to me, have you? I shall never forgive him!' 'Don't try to be funny either. His name's not George. Is it?' The last bit he addressed to me, and he had this anxious note in his voice, as if he'd just sung 'Happy Birthday' to someone and now it might have been the wrong person or the wrong day. 'It's all right,' I said, 'it's just a little joke, something we have between us.' Jeannie couldn't leave it alone, though. 'What makes you so sure his name isn't George? What's wrong with the name George? There are perfectly decent people called George.' 'I didn't say anything was wrong with it. I just said it wasn't his name.' 'How do you know that?' 'How do I know his name isn't George? I just do.' 'How do you?' 'Look, I told you to shut up.' 'Me?' 'Yes, I told you to shut up, so shut up.' She's sitting there all injured innocence at this point, with her hand flat on her chest and I think that's the moment he notices that she's got nothing on under her sweater because her nipples are showing quite distinctly through the wool. He gives a funny little twitch. 'You think it's all a joke, don't you?' he says. 'People like you think everything's a joke. Well, you've got to be taught different. You'd be surprised to hear that there are some decent people in the world, people who don't behave the way you do, people who'd be ashamed to talk the way you talk.' 'People who talk the way you talk you mean?' she asks in a very serious voice, like she was interviewing someone on the box and wanted to get it perfectly straight for the benefit of the viewers. 'How I talk is neither here nor there. I advise you to listen to what I say because you are on dangerous ground. Extremely dangerous ground.' She sits there, both hands flat on the carpet behind her, arms braced, chin up with a this-promises-to-be-a-more-interesting-experience-than-I-thought expression on her face. 'Have you ever considered how his wife feels? Have you ever considered how she feels?' 'Yes,' she said, 'I have actually. From all that I gather she feels a lot happier.' 'That's the most disgusting thing I've ever heard anyone say. Would you like to know what you are?' 'I thought I was the Whore of Babylon. Aren't I?' 'You're a thief, that's what you are, a thief.' 'And what are you, if I may ask?' 'We're talking about you. Never mind me. You know what happens to thieves? Do you?' 'About fifty-three per cent of them get away with it, as far as I remember.' 'And this is the woman you're willing to deceive your wife with, is it? A thief. Someone who takes what doesn't belong to her.' 'People don't belong to people. Slavery's been abolished, in case you hadn't heard, because that's what you're talking about. Slavery. People don't belong to other people.' 'I'm not talking about that aspect.' 'Oh. I beg your pardon.'

'I'm not talking about trying to get people to break their promises. I'm talking about asking a man to desert his hearth and home—' 'George, answer me truthfully now, have I ever asked you to desert your hearth and home?' I didn't like to answer, even as a joke, because somehow I didn't find it funny, I felt a bit ashamed actually. 'You're not only wicked, your sort of woman, you're shameless as well. You don't know what shame is.' 'You come in here, waving a gun, and tell me about having no shame? How dare you? Honestly!' 'Those whom the Lord hath brought together let no man put asunder, what do you say to that?' 'First of all I'm not putting anyone asunder, secondly I don't believe in the Lord and thirdly I'm not at all certain that it's an accurate quotation.' 'Not an accurate quotation? What do you mean by that? It's from the wedding ceremony.' 'Ah then it must be accurate.' 'As for believing in the Lord, I don't suppose you do. Can't afford to, can you?' 'Would you explain to me why it's all right to come and terrorize people with guns and wrong to make love when you want to?' 'I'll tell you what your idea of love is, you don't know what love is, you think it's filth and corruption and lying about the place, and it's not that at all, not by a long chalk.' 'In that case, I wish you'd enlighten us.' 'You need to be taken down a peg. You need to be humbled in my opinion. You need to be made to see the error of your ways.' 'And who, may I ask, are you to tell me what I need, apart from a stupid little man with a gun in his hand?' 'Stupid, am I?' 'I don't think he's stupid, Jeannie, I don't think you should say that. I think he may be quite right. Maybe we should see the error of our ways.' I expected to collect a pat on the head for that, but he turned and looked at me and if I ever

saw NOTHING written on a man's face in capital letters, it
was then. Talk about 'This space to let'. Finally he pressed
his lips together and nodded a couple of times as much as to
say, hard cases, long job. The next thing he said was the last
thing I expected, which was, 'Take off your sweater. Take
off your sweater,' he said, 'do as I say.' 'I don't want to,'
Jeannie said, 'it's cold.' 'No, it's not. Take it off when I tell
you to.' She looks at me and I think, Christ, I've got to do
something. She expects me to do something, but what can
I do? I promise you, it looks as though the gun's grown two
inches at least, in the interim, sweet peas after a shower.
'No, pull it up over your face,' he says, 'just pull it up over
your face. Never mind taking it off.' She looks at me and I
can see she blames me. There's tears in her eyes suddenly,
and of course I'm to blame. I can understand how she feels,
obviously, but there's absolutely nothing I can do that I
can see, not for the moment. 'You'd better do as I say.' And
so she does, with a look at the two of us as if she can't decide
which of us she hates more, she lifts up her sweater, arms
crossed over each other as if she was going to pull it right
off, and he gives this funny smile and it's all I can do not to
smile back, I know it sounds awful, but it's as if he was
saying you must admit this bit's all right, you must grant me
that much. He moves a little closer to her and smiles again.
He moves closer but without putting one foot in front of the
other, with a kind of shuffle, and he just stares at her breasts.
'O.K., just like that,' he whispers. And then he winks at me.
He winks at me and that turns my stomach and I have to
look away and when I look back he's got his hand halfway
towards her tit. I want to say, 'Nice, aren't they?' to try and
get him into a better frame of mind, but I don't like to in

case Jeannie doesn't see it like that, in case she thinks I'm laughing at her, ganging up on her, which I now have no inclination to do whatsoever. It was as if his arm was too short for what he wanted to do, as if he couldn't reach as far as he wanted to; at the same time it was as if his fingers were breathing and she could feel the breath of them on her skin, because she sort of shivered, and moved and her breast swung and, Christ, the blood came in my throat and I felt such love for her, this faceless girl as she was at that moment, I could have strangled him. She was trying to get the sweater right over her head now, she felt trapped obviously and scared and wanted to see what was going on, and as she moved, her breast nudged his hand and she reared back like someone in a game and he reached and put his hand right across her face, pressed the wool into her face, as if he wanted to gag her. She still had her glasses on and the points of the frame stuck out, just above his hand, and you could see the lenses and it was like she'd been blinded, she was some funny kind of a blinded animal. He held her like that and then he smiled at me and there was just the two of us, no one moved now, us two and these two naked breasts, queer. The sweater was getting wet where her mouth was. I didn't like that. He said, 'Now let's get this straight, shall we? You're never going to see each other again, ever.' 'If you say so,' I said. 'Whatever you say.' He stared at me, the gun pointing straight at me, I didn't like the silence one bit, I thought Christ what a farce he's going to pull the trigger because he can't think of anything else to do, what a farce! 'I'll promise if you like,' I said. He just looked at me and then he looked down at her, like you do at a child to make sure it's asleep before you say something you don't particularly want it to hear, and he took a sort of half step towards me, leaving his hand over her face. 'Here,' he said, 'tell me something. Is there anything you'd really like to do to her?' I felt sick, and he realized. He took his hand off her face and it hung in the air, as if he wasn't sure whether it was fit to use or not. 'I only thought—' 'Look,' I said, 'what I'd really like to do is get her home and call it a day.' 'What do you mean home exactly?' 'I want to take her to where she lives, that's what I mean.' 'Why don't you take her home with you and show her to your wife and children while you're at it?' 'And what good will that do?' 'There's nothing you wouldn't do if it got you out of a jam, is there?' 'Listen, you've had your fun—' 'Fun? Did you say fun?' 'I've got a few quid in my pocket, why don't you take that and—?' 'Do you think money's all I care about? Do you think money's all I care about? Do you think that's why I'm here?' 'Why are you here if it isn't money?' 'Lie down on your face. Go on, on your face, do as I say.' He loved saying that, he'd probably never given anyone orders before. 'Face down, chew the carpet, go on, do as I say, hands behind your neck and don't move or you'll get something you don't particularly want.' All I could assume was he wanted to mess Jeannie about. I wasn't worried about myself, but I thought if he starts messing her about, I don't know what I'll do but I'll have to do something. I never seriously imagined he'd shoot me just like that. I think he was too glad of my company, as a matter of fact, to do a thing like that. So there he was, face to face with Jeannie, except he hadn't left her a face, properly speaking. I put my face down in the Axminster, but slightly to one side, so I could just see out of the corner of my eye what he was doing. She stayed still as a dummy and I thought of those women in Amsterdam and how you wondered how they can just sit there in the windows of their hutches and let men's eyes paw them all over, it seems worse than what comes after honestly, just sitting there. On the other hand, I now sort of understood because I didn't feel anything and I could imagine Jeannie didn't. I saw how you could go so passive on a situation it just didn't mean anything any more, rape, death, anything. Once there's no alternative you just accept it and somehow at the same moment you feel completely free, free to go anywhere, think of anything you like, it's a kind of drunkenness, when you're as low as a human being can be, you're suddenly like a king, you're beyond worrying, you feel quite light-headed and whoever's on top of you, you can laugh at them because they're more the slaves of their own power than you are even. It's really true. I felt like we were playing games with a kid before his bath time, I felt no more afraid than if his gun had been made of licorice. He had us there, he could do what he liked with us, and at the same time I felt as if he was completely dependent on us and we were only humouring him. I must've closed my eyes – do you know, I honestly think perhaps I dozed off for a second or two? – anyway, next time I looked he wasn't near Jeannie at all. I think he fancied a good feel, you know, but he'd lost his nerve. He was wandering round the room and finally he comes round the other side of me and I can see his feet, about two yards in front of me. 'So this is where you work, is it?' I mumbled something into the carpet, making it deliberately unintelligible. He said, 'All right, you can come up, only slowly mind, nice and slowly.' I came up like I was doing the Canadian Air Force exercises because it's no good doing

148

them too fast, you don't get the benefit. (Same with the Isometric.) 'O.K., that'll do, hands behind your neck, do as I say.' He backed off once I was settled and went to the secretary's desk. 'No expense spared I must say.' He took a jotter off the desk and a black Pentel from the rack and sat on the edge of the desk and wrote something. I hate the squeak of those things when someone else uses them, gives me the shivers. He had a bit of a time, trying to write and keep the gun pointed at me, I thought he was going to drop it at one point, the gun, and I almost lurched forward, instinctively, to pick it up for him and he shot me a look, but not unfriendly, as much as to say no you don't, but thanks all the same. Finally he brought the pad over and showed it to me. Do you know what he'd written? 'Do you love her?' Passing messages in class, that was what he was doing. 'What's this say then?' I said, because it wasn't particularly good writing. 'You know,' he said. 'Oh yes,' I said, 'I can read it now. Do I love her?' He looked a bit wounded at that, a bit sulky, he'd probably guessed I'd deliberately said it out loud to keep Jeannie in the picture, which was not what he wanted. 'Yes,' I said, 'I do, as a matter of fact.' And I thought, he's a funny bloke to get married by, because it suddenly occurred to me he'd put the question to me in a sort of formal way that put me in mind of a clergyman sort of thing. At the same time I completely lost this feeling I'd previously had about him, that we sort of had something in common. I felt completely disgusted by him, making her sit with her tits hanging out, it wasn't funny any more. It was horrible. I said, 'Look, you can't leave her like that, she can't breathe properly. It's inhuman.'

'So?'

'So it's inhuman.'

'And what're you prepared to do about it?'

'I'm prepared to help her put her sweater back where it belongs.'

'Try it.'

'Look, have a bit of common sense, for God's sake.'

'Did you say God?' He was all set to shoot me suddenly, I could see that.

'You're going to damage her health, leaving her sitting like that.' It was actually getting a lot colder for some reason. It must've been the time switch. The heating had gone off and the place was cooling down. It'd be a funny thing, wouldn't it, to be found frozen to death in the executive suite when the cleaner arrived in the morning? Her breasts were going a sort of mottled colour which was the reverse of stimulating actually. 'You can't leave her like that.'

'And I want to know what you're willing to do about it.'

'Do you really think you have a right to damage her health? Because that's what you're doing. The girl's cold, you can see that.'

'O.K.,' he said finally, 'O.K. Not that it makes any difference, but you can put your sweater down if you want to.'

She did, and I was all set to welcome her back into the room, it was as if she'd come back into the room and we were involved in some conversation, me and this other bloke, the tail end of some business she wasn't too interested in, and I wanted to tip her the wink we wouldn't be long, we'd be with her in a minute, when she gave me this look as if she hated me more than she did old Murgatroyd. Her face was all raw-looking, you could see the veins round her eyes and she looked properly furious and nothing like as pretty as I'd remembered, I was quite disappointed. I thought Christ this is a fine time to get huffy because here I am doing my best, at least I've got your face back for you, and all you can do is look at me as if I'd brought my tapeworm home to dinner. Instead of being this girl I had on the side I felt as if we were married, as if this bloke had gone and hooked us together, and I was in trouble with the wife, as usual.

He said, 'You've got never to see each other again.'

'So you said.'

'Look, you'd better watch it or you'll be back where you were just now.'

'We won't,' she said, 'ever.' She sounded as if she meant it too. 'Will we?'

'Absolutely not.' I meant it and all. I honestly wondered what the hell we could want to see each other for. She looked like ice. It seemed a million years since she'd hooked her leg over the back of the big buttoned sofa and said, 'Straight on for paradise, sailor.'

'Ah but how can I be sure?'

'That is a problem. I think you'll have to watch us, won't you?'

Jeannie didn't like me saying that.

'Watch you? How can I watch you? I can't watch you. And I've got to be sure. I've got to be sure before I leave this room that you won't ever see each other again.' There was a silence and we looked at each other, Jeannie and me, like two players going for the same ball, two players on the same side, and there was a sort of anger between us that didn't have anything in common with the anger two people on opposite sides feel for each other, because there was fear in it too, fear of what was going to be said afterwards, fear of what was going to show on the action replay and who was going to blame the other for what happened and neither of them can change.

Office Procedure.

'We could promise,' I said.

'Promise could you? When did you last keep a promise?'

'Who says I don't keep my promises?' I tried to sound as if he'd really pushed it too far this time, as if now we really had a reason for quarrelling. Jeannie believed me even if he didn't, that I was willing to promise, because she was looking at me as if I was a meat pie with a mouse inside.

'When did you last keep a promise I should like to know? You talk about keeping promises when you've married one person and then start carrying on with another? And what did you promise her, what did you have to promise her, while you're at it?'

'Promise her? I didn't promise her anything. I don't know what you're talking about.'

'To get her to let you do what you wanted.'

'You're joking.'

'I don't joke about that sort of thing.'

'Oh, what sort of thing do you joke about?' It was the sort of remark I thought Jeannie might appreciate, the sort of thing she might have said herself as a matter of fact, but her whole attitude seemed to have changed, she just looked away and I could imagine her thinking 'illiterate' because that was what she looked like and I thought fuck you, in the middle of all this. If she wanted a divorce, she could have one.

'You're not suggesting she just offered herself to you, are you?'

'Yes, as a matter of fact, she came in on the tea trolley.'

'Look—' and he wagged the gun.

'Tell me something,' I said, 'have you ever had anything to do with women? Honestly now.'

'I'm not here to answer questions.'

'Well, what are you here for?'

'I would have thought you'd've realized by now.'

'What's your name?'

'My name?'

'Yes.'

'I'm not telling you my name.'

'Why not? I'd like to know.'

'I wouldn't be very clever telling you that, would I?'

I thought, well, that's something, because he obviously expects us to survive this, otherwise he wouldn't be so cautious.

'What's important is what I represent, isn't it?'

'What you represent.'

'Which is justice in a way.'

'Ah.'

'That's what I represent. I don't have to have a name.' It was a sort of afterthought, but he seemed quite stunned when he'd said it. It was as if he'd always been called something ridiculous like Snodgrass or Winterbottom or had the initials W.C. or V.D. or something and suddenly he didn't have to answer to it any more, suddenly he was liberated. I looked at my watch and I gave Jeannie a little nod and then when he saw it, as I meant him to do, I flinched and looked away as if I'd blown a secret. 'Here, what's going on?

I saw that. What's going on? Come on.' He was glaring at her and she looked over at me, really desperate for a second, because of all the things she hated, not understanding was the worst. She hated to feel out of something. Only he got the impression from the way she looked at me that she was the one holding out on him and that made him concentrate on her all the more. I felt as if I'd done something really clever, as if I'd really brought something off. The thing being that he wanted to get something out of her that she hadn't really got. I felt I'd delivered her up to him and at the same time put him on a false scent, collision course, if you see what I mean. And meanwhile I was in the clear.

'What was he trying to tell you? I want to know.'

'I haven't the faintest idea.'

I said, 'Come on, Jeannie, might as well tell him.'

He smirked and said, 'Very sensible of you.'

'Don't you think so?'

She said, 'I don't know what you're talking about.'

I said, 'Seriously, we might as well—'

She scrambled up and onto the sofa.

'Who said you could move?'

'I want a cigarette.'

'Well, you can't have one.'

She clicked her tongue.

I said, 'I may as well tell you. They come round at midnight.'

She tucked her mouth to one side, as if to say, you might have thought of something better than that. Critic.

'Who do?'

'The security people.'

'Midnight you say. That's not for a bit yet, is it?'

154

'They might come sooner. I don't know.'

'Don't you? I think you do. They won't come before midnight if that's when they're supposed to come.'

'They don't keep to a strict timetable, do they? For obvious reasons.'

'Think I don't know? You're not going to trick me, so don't try.'

'I'm not.'

'Because it won't work.'

'Look, I didn't have to tell you.' All the while I'm trying to re-establish contact with Jeannie, make her realize I'm doing my best to get him in two minds, because that's the ideal thing, get them in two minds, only she seemed to have got tired of the whole thing. She was sitting there looking the other way, like him and me were two drunks in a train and all she could do was wait for us to get off. I thought you fat cow, aren't you, you won't give me the benefit of the doubt if it kills you.

'Mrs Hanson?'

'Have you got a car?' I said.

'Do I own a car?'

'Here. Have you got a car here?'

'That's my affair, isn't it?'

'I was wondering how you got here.'

'I'm here, that's what matters.'

'Agreed. But what made you come? It's a long way from anywhere.'

'I came, that's what matters.'

'I never heard you arrive.'

'Ah well, there we are.'

'Tricks of the trade.'

'If you like.'

'He walked.'

'Did I? Who said? I didn't as a matter of fact.'

'Maybe he flew,' Jeannie said.

'I came on my moped as a matter of fact.' He came out with it just like that, and very dignified. 'Stop laughing. Stop laughing, both of you, or I'll—'

'Shoot us?'

'I'm warning you.'

'For *laughing*. Is that your idea of justice you're so proud of?' Jeannie was furious suddenly, but I could see him riding on his moped, with this gun in his mac pocket. And wearing his peaked crash helmet: it was too much. It was all I could do not to burst out laughing again.

'You think anyone who hasn't got a car is funny. Well, plenty of people haven't got cars and they're just as good as you, just as good, if not better, so—' and he wagged the gun again.

I said, 'If you'll just go home now I swear to you we won't ever mention this evening to a living soul.'

'You've got a hope. I'm not just packing up and going home, not by a long chalk.'

'Are you enjoying yourself?'

'I beg your pardon?'

'I said, are you enjoying yourself?' She was back in the game, old Jeannie, and I was glad to have her.

'In a way,' he said, but sullenly, as if it was an unfair question and no one had intervened to protect him.

'Anything's better than being on your own, isn't it?'

'I don't know how many times I've got to tell you—'

'Do you really want us not to speak, really?'

'I said so, didn't I?'

Jeannie said, 'Has anyone ever loved you?'

'Apart from your mother.'

'If you had one.'

'You fucking cow,' he said. 'You fucking cow.'

'Thank you.'

Bogged it, I thought. Pity. We had him going there for a second. Choose the wrong moment to be clever. Pity. I cleared my throat. 'Look,' I said, 'you've given us a hell of a fright, no question about it. If that's what you set out to do, you've succeeded. I don't think I shall ever quite be the same again. Seriously, you've made quite an impression. As a result, I'm being perfectly honest now, I find it quite difficult to think of you as just another human being. And I expect you have the same feeling about us.'

'Do I?'

'I think you probably do. Only now—you know you said my name wasn't George. You guessed it wasn't George. Well, I want to tell you what it is and Jeannie, I want you to tell him what your name is. My name's Charlie Hanson.'

'And I'm Jean Haughton.' Good girl.

'What're you trying to do?'

'What's yours?'

'Oh no.'

'All right, if you're frightened.'

'Frightened? I'm not frightened. I'm just not that easily tricked. Not by a long chalk. What makes you think I'm frightened?'

'O.K., then let's concentrate on us. Because we're just

a pair of ordinary people. You think we're something terrible, but we're really not. We haven't really done anything so awful either.'

'Seriously,' Jeannie said. 'Why do you think sex is so wicked?'

'I didn't say it was, I said you were—'

'But you do, you must. You wouldn't have objected if we'd been drinking together, or filing the mail, or—you *do*—' she spoke very gently, as if she was trying to get a kid to give back something that didn't belong to it. 'Don't you? And it's so silly—'

'Why do you hide it, what you do, if there's nothing wrong with it?'

'Men are such hypocrites,' Jeannie said. 'That's partly why. And just because it isn't wrong doesn't mean you have to go waving it around in public, does it? Please try to understand.'

'I know what you're thinking. You're thinking what a joke this is, what a joke it'll be once I've gone and you can laugh about it.'

'Is that what's worrying you?'

'No, it's not worrying me. You think I'm afraid to shoot, don't you? But I'm not.'

'If we thought that,' I said, 'do you think we'd've waited this long before trying to jump you? What I'd like to know is why life is so unimportant to you, why you're so afraid of it. Because being willing to shoot us, when let's face it we've done nothing to you, it's equivalent to being willing to shoot yourself really, isn't it?'

'You think shooting someone else is the same as shooting yourself? You won't think that when it happens.'

'What I mean is, you don't like life basically. It worries you. Imagine if you shot us, what kind of a life would you be able to lead afterwards? You'd never be able to lead a normal life again. Finish ours and you'll finish your own, that's what I mean. And it's true, isn't it? If you think it out.'

'Ours? What do you mean ours? You're two entirely separate people. As you'll soon realize.'

SHAVERS ONLY.

Jeannie said, 'Please, sir, can I be excused?'
'What're you talking about?'
'I need to take a pee.'
'Well, you can't.'
'I have to.'
'Well, you can't.'
'What do you want me to do? It's only down the passage.'
'I'm not bothered where it is. You can't.'
'I've got to.'
I didn't like to look at her. Frankly, I was a bit divided; I suppose she really did want to go, but when you think how long a woman can wait in the normal course, I couldn't help feeling that she was deliberately making difficulties, trying to embarrass him and I sort of understood his side. She was playing on his conscience, which was fair enough, but somehow embarrassing him was something else again. I said, 'There's one off Lambert's office. Through there.' It wouldn't do for the top man to be seen to be needing a leak. She looked at me as if I'd wrecked the whole thing. Old Murgatroyd said, 'Why didn't you say there was one in there?' 'I forgot.' 'Forgot? Expect me to believe that?' 'I de-

liberately forgot,' Jeannie said. 'Deliberately forgot? That's not possible.' 'Ah.' 'Deliberately forgetting.' 'Well, then.' 'All right,' he said, 'go. Go on. Go. Only you'd better come back. Because if you don't, if there's any trouble, any hitch, he gets it. In the head.' 'You're nice, aren't you?' 'Never mind what I am. I'm telling you. You go and you come back. Otherwise ... ' 'And you lecture us about morals.' She despised him, she really did. 'In the head, don't say I didn't warn you.' 'Look, I'm only going to pee.' 'All right.' It disgusted him, and she knew it, her talking like that, and I thought what a coward he was, I mean literally, how he was afraid of things, and then I remembered how I used to hate hearing Lo drop a big one in case it put me off and I thought, Oh brother! How we hate women to be real, really, when it comes to it we want them to be another race, we want them to be differently constituted from us. We want them to be soft and then again we want them to be hard as hell. Have you noticed how often a bloke'll lose his temper with his missus as soon as she has something the smallest bit wrong with her? She's only got to develop a limp or ask him to feel a bump she's got on her leg and he's completely out of control, he's furious. Why is that? The fact is he thinks she owes it to him to be in good nick. If anything goes wrong it's like she's supposed to be under guarantee and basically what he'd like to do is send her back to the makers with a complaint. A woman's not supposed to go wrong, she's supposed to give reliable service or you've got a legitimate right to your money back. On the other hand, when a man's sick for any reason, even when it's only a runny nose (which is hideous on a woman), she's forever running after you with Kleenex and home-made soup and something her mother always used to do for people with whatever you've got. And then she wants to know where did you pick it up and who were you with, when what does it matter, and all you want is two aspirin and a bit of quiet. I often think they actually look forward to you being sick, they don't really feel, deep down, they're getting their money's worth when you're fit and running about. They only feel fulfilled when you're flat on your back and they're shaking down the old thermometer. A man's not like that, even when he's really keen on someone, she's only got to have a drip on the end of her nose and he's wondering how he ever got into this mess. Basically a man doesn't want to know about a woman being human, certainly he doesn't want to know about how like him she is, that above all. Women want recognition as human beings, obviously, because who wants to feel excluded, but we don't want to give it to them if we can help it. Now put it that way and it's wrong to deny them, obviously, but what they have to face is, if they achieve recognition, and I grant you it's bound to come, in say twenty years, we shan't want to know about them, we shall treat them much worse than we do now. Why? Because the mystery'll be gone, won't it? Admit they're much the same as we are and who's going to bother with them? The world's run on guilt, basically, take that away and put honesty in its place and you're going to have a lot more misery than you do at present. We're nice to women as much as we are, because we know we're getting away with it, we're getting away with murder, I'm not denying that, but give them their rights, give them their equality, admit there's no real difference between the sexes and everyone's got a right to do and be what he wants and I reckon you'll get the reverse of what you think you'll get, you'll get fights and rapes and stand-up rows, you'll get all kinds of trouble. They think we think they're inferior, we treat them like inferior beings, but that's only part of it. It so happens we also worship them, although naturally we don't say so. We really believe they have qualities we don't and we worship them accordingly, but only when they deliver the goods because that's what Gods are all about, and that includes naturally enough not sneezing all over us or telling us about their ankles.

'She's being a hell of a time.'

'She'd better come back. I meant what I said. I hope she doesn't take advantage.'

'So do I.' I smiled at him, as much as to say that I understood his position, even if she didn't. I recognized his authority. It was like smiling at a policeman.

He said, 'Tell me the truth. What's the difference between this woman and any other? Really.' 'She's pretty, she's nice to look at, she's attractive.' 'So're lots of women. What about your wife?' 'That's not the same.' 'Never mind, what's the difference really?' 'The difference is, she's different.' 'That's playing with words, that's just being clever.' 'All right, she's the one who happened to present herself. After all, you can't just go round the world and pick any woman you want, can you? You have to see what comes along.' 'And she came along.' 'Roughly.' 'And that's worth risking your life for?' 'To be perfectly honest, it didn't occur to me that I was. You're not exactly the sort of thing that happens every day, are you?' 'Potentially,' he said. 'I hope she's all right,' I said, 'I hope she's not sick.' He looked at his watch. 'How much longer before you shoot me?' 'You'd better not joke about

it.' 'I'm not.' 'Because I meant it.' 'I know.' 'You think I'm
joking, but I'm not. Do you really love her, this woman,
really?' 'Why?' 'I'm asking you. Do you?' I wished she'd
come back. What the hell was she up to? 'Come on, I want
an answer.' 'I don't know,' I said, 'I don't know if I've ever
loved anybody. That's not true. Sometimes I'm sure I do,
you can't help it, can you, at times? But that's usually
because they make you feel so good, it's just an extra bit of
getting what you want from them. You can't hug yourself,
kind of thing, so you hug them instead. Do you know what
I mean?' He just stared at me. He seemed to be dreaming. I
said, 'You've been inside, haven't you?' It occurred to me
perhaps she really had skipped, old Jeannie, and I'd better
play for time any way I could. I thought what a calculating
little cow, just to skip like that and leave me to take my
chances, and on the other hand she was absolutely right
because she could hardly ask for permission, could she?
Still, how was she going to face me if I got out of it, I
wondered. Cool as you like, in all probability, 'Good
morning, Mr Hanson,' and still telling the typists like that
little Lily that I was illiterate – more illiterate than ever I
daresay because a bad conscience doesn't exactly make you
generous in circumstances like that. 'I don't get you,' he
said. 'Inside. You've done time, haven't you? Bird, haven't
you?' 'That's my business.' 'Quite. You've done time and
that's made you how you are.' 'How I am is my business.'
He'd shrunk, except for the gun, he seemed like such a little
bloke, wrong diet probably. 'And that's why you're jealous,
I mean, because you've been done out of your life, or a bit of
it, and it's made you jealous.' 'What have I got to be jealous
about?' 'Look, be honest. Me and this girl, wherever she

163

is—' I thought if I drew attention to her absence myself he'd be less likely to go potty and do something stupid. What I mean is, I didn't want him suddenly to think he was late for the office and shoot me because he'd missed his train. 'She'd better not be doing anything funny.' 'You're telling me.' 'Can you trust her?' 'Can you ever trust a woman?' 'That's a funny thing for you to be saying. After the way you behave.' I said, 'You've never had it properly yourself, have you, at all?' 'Had what?' 'You know.' 'Had what?' 'Why hedge? You haven't, have you? A woman. I promise I won't laugh—' '*You* promise? *You* promise? Christ! you'd better be careful, you had.' I thought of God, I swear I did. He looked that terrible for a moment, and pathetic all at the same time. I felt sorry for him. I thought of God and how even when He had a Son, if you believe all that stuff, He had to get the Holy Ghost to give Mary A.I.D. Poor old omnipotent bastard honestly. 'You've never had a woman in your life, have you, why not admit it?' 'I warn you—' 'And as a result you think it's something enormous, in itself, something frightful, beyond your imagination—' 'You're taking a lot on yourself, you're taking a great deal on yourself.' 'You think—' 'Shut up.' 'Let me talk,' I actually shouted at him, 'let me talk. Why don't you want people to talk to you? Tell me something, doesn't it ever occur to you that people take advantage of you? They take advantage of you all the time, don't they? Who told you to come here? Someone did, didn't they?' 'Look, this is loaded.' 'God, I hope so,' I said. I had to laugh and he did too, in a crooked little way, like a man with brown teeth, who smiles and keeps his lips pressed together at the same time. 'I'd like to help you,' I said, 'believe it or not. I feel something for you, I do truly.'

164

'You're in a hole and you're trying to get out of it. You don't fool me. You're trying to get round me, that's all, and it's not going to wash.' 'But why not? Why not? Why not let it? I promise you I won't— I don't know how to put it — I won't take advantage.' 'Yes, you will,' he said, and he did sound sad. 'Yes, you will.' There wasn't half a banging going on. He looked at me and with such hatred it turned my stomach. 'You think you've been very clever, don't you?' And his finger was tightening. I wondered how much leeway there was, because I could see it tightening, and then we heard Jeannie's shouting, 'Oy, oy.' She sounded quite narked. A woman hates to be ignored. 'Get in there.' I went into Lambert's office and he followed and shut the door behind us. There was double doors into Lambert's bog, with a sort of vestibule between the two, with a basin and a cupboard in it, and consequently we hadn't heard Jeannie calling. Would you believe it? She'd gone and locked herself in the bog. 'What the hell's she think she's playing at?' 'I don't know,' I said. I think we were both as annoyed as each other. I opened the outer door and said, 'What's the trouble?' 'I don't know how it works,' she said, 'I managed to lock it, but I can't undo the damned thing.' It was one of these knobs you lock without a key, by pressing it in and twisting it round and now she didn't know how to undo it. Old Murg was worried we'd get so close to each other, him and me, that I'd be able to jump him, so he hung back in the office and gestured me to go and help. 'I don't know what to do.' 'Go on.' 'I've never sat on Mr Livingston's throne,' I said, 'I don't know what to do.' 'Tell her what she's supposed to do. And don't try shutting this door, because this goes right through doors.' 'I suppose in that case we could always shoot the lock off the bog,' I said, 'if the worst comes to the worst. After all, we don't want the fire brigade, do we?' 'We're not having the fire brigade.' 'It won't turn.' Oh shut up, I thought, why can't you? Frankly I'd rather come to the conclusion that she really had scarpered somehow or other and my whole conversation with old Murg was rather cunningly angled to making it too late for him to shoot me, to putting us both somehow on the same side of the fence with regard to women and life and consequently depriving him of the climax which he'd obviously need to make him pull the trigger. And now here she was back again. I only realized when she drew attention to herself what a bloody nuisance it was she was still on the premises. In other words, it was only after the event that I saw what I'd been up to. Which is typical of life, isn't it? I thought silly bitch locks herself in the bog and here was I thinking she was over the hills and far away. 'What did you do when you locked it in the first place?' I tried to talk to her in my normal voice, as if Murg weren't there, but I was amazed how annoyed I sounded, even though I did my best to put on a good show, for him principally, of being a decent ordinary affectionate bloke. 'I just pushed the knob and twisted the little sort of thing on the top.' 'Well push it in again and twist it back.' 'I've tried that.' 'Twist the whole knob then.' 'I've tried that too.' 'Try pushing it in and twisting the knob at the same time, with two hands.' 'It's no good.' 'Well, it looks as if that's where you'll be spending the night then, doesn't it?' 'Tell her, she'd better come out.' 'Our friend says you'd better come out.' 'Thanks a lot.' 'There isn't a window, is there?' 'Look, no messing about—' 'Yes and a five floor drop.' 'That's no good then.' You know

166

what I did? I caught hold of the knob and tried it and the door opened. She must've unlocked it without realizing one of the times and she'd been so defeatist she hadn't realized. I backed out in front of her and out she came. She must've tarted herself up because she looked quite rested, quite chipper, and I thought Christ, you've overdone it a bit, the make-up. She smiled at me as if she'd at least kept her word, as if she'd done something really praiseworthy, like a secretary who comes in and thinks she's done you a favour bailing you out of some dreary meeting and actually she's gone and spiked a promising development. I really think I could've come to some arrangement with him if she'd had the wit to make herself scarce. All I could think was, trust you.

'I tried the office.'

The phone was ringing. It was ringing in the same room we were in but it must have rung three times at least before any of us registered. Jeannie must've taken half a step to it (well trained) before Murg had his gun on her. 'Touch it, you try. Touch it and you're dead.' This time I believed him. He was whispering very dramatically, as if someone were trying the door, as if the person who was calling only needed to have the receiver taken off and he'd pop up like a jack-in-the-box fully armed, or he was hiding in the desk drawer. Obviously what happened was, Lambert had the phone switched through to his office when the switchboard girl went off home and someone must've tried the office, though I don't know who they hoped to get at that hour, and of course it had rung in Lambert's office. It couldn't have happened at a worse moment frankly. I really thought in spite of Jeannie we had old Murg going but now I could see him receding like a rescue ship in a storm. It stopped ringing after a while and there was a silence as if a bomb was going to go off. We were all waiting for it to go again. I said, 'It might—' But he had the gun up like a flash and he wasn't joking. He was panting again, like when he'd first come in. I was that pissed off I could've spat. And probably it was a wrong number at that. He was going through the drawers of the desk, pulling them out leaving them open and then banging them because he did it from the top down and of course he couldn't see into the bottom ones because the top ones were in the way. No method. 'Are you looking for something?' 'You'll see.' We were standing around like passengers who've had their flight called but haven't been told which gate number. Finally he gave up the desk and went over to the bureau affair. They always have one, don't they, these executives, one of those double-fronted jobs with Chinese trees on the doors? It's like the fire extinguisher; I reckon these blokes who sell fire extinguishers must put the fear of God into these top executives because they always have one, it's like the three-gallon ash-tray, essential equipment. Whatever he was looking for he didn't find, so he went over to the window and looked between the curtains. Then he put his hand in his pocket and brought out a pen-knife, just a single blade with a wooden shield and he opened it and then he held it out to me. 'Come on, over here.' He came towards me and sort of passed this little knife to me as if it was the baton in a relay or something. He left me standing with it and he was over by Jeannie. He sat on the desk with Jeannie sort of beside him and the gun by her body and then he said, 'Cut the strings off the curtains. And make them as long as you can.' I didn't get what he meant for a moment. I looked and then I frowned at him. 'The curtain strings.' He sort of blushed, as if he was afraid he'd used the wrong expression. 'And no messing about, or you know what happens to her.' They were together by the lamp, both of them looking at me. I might have been a photographer or somebody about to take their picture, the way they looked, side by side but very tense, waiting. 'As long as you can make them,' he said, 'and no messing about.' He always felt better when he'd said something twice.

'Can you describe him for us?'
'Do you know it's very difficult?'
'Would you say he was dark?'
'Mousey, I suppose you'd call him. Size eight in shoes. Sixteen collar. About five foot nine.'
'Any scars or anything like that? Moustache?'
'No, nothing like that. Reasonable-looking. Rather a pasty face, yellowish complexion, brown eyes, what more can I tell you? Amazing, isn't it, to spend that much time with someone and be so vague?'
'I think the best thing would probably be if we came round.'
'Of course, if you want to, only what for? I mean — '
'Well, if we're going to try and find somebody we shall need something a bit more precise than you've given us — '
'Oh I see what you mean.'
'I presume you've got a photograph.'
'Of my husband.'

'Well, that's who we're talking about, isn't it?'
'Yes, of course, I'm sorry.'

'Now tie him up.'
'Please—'
'Tie him up.'
'Couldn't you let us go now? Please.'
'I told you to tie him up.'
'What if I refuse?'
'I wouldn't if I was you.'
'Wouldn't you? Are you sure? Imagine if you were me.'
'No one's going to hear, you know.'
'Jeannie, do as he says, go on, do as he says.'
'Charlie, shut up, shut up. I can't, I can't.'
'I can't help you, so you'll have to.' He sounded quite apologetic.
'I promise you we'll never see each other again.'
'We've been through that.'
'If you're serious about not wanting us to.'
'I'll leave my job, if you like,' I said, because I could tell Jeannie wasn't playing about. She'd come to the end of her tether, just like that, bang. I was trying to be the reasonable one, anxious to make a deal, a sort of professional conciliator, you might say, which did after all happen to be my job in real life.

'Lie down on the ground, like I told you, and get your hands behind your back and don't move again unless I tell you to.'

I braced my shoulders apart and made the angle as wide as possible between my wrists, that much I did do, but here's the funny thing, when I felt the cords drop onto my wrists,

I was lying on the floor face down, on the Axminster, and as I felt the cords, they were nylon, so they were unexpectedly cool, I immediately felt this sexual excitement. I mean it was unmistakable. I was quite taken by surprise, but there was no question about it. I mean, you either are or you aren't, aren't you, excited? And I was.

'Do the feet first,' he said. 'Go on.' Something had obviously occurred to him. 'Leave that and do the feet.'

What I did for the feet was I kept my legs side by side as far as I could, so that she looped the cord over the full extent of both legs. They were together, but not overlapping and in that way I thought I'd be able to find a bit of slack in the rope when the time came, though of course I didn't have the foggiest when that would be. Well finally I was all roped up and waiting for British Rail, and as you know that can be quite a long wait. I was reconciled to it as a matter of fact. I felt quite cosy. The ropes were smooth, they didn't rub my wrists or anything, and already I was making a bit of slack, the knots weren't too hot, even though he'd stood over her when she tied them and given them a bit of a yank himself with his foot in the small of my back which I didn't appreciate.

'We haven't done anything to you,' Jeannie said. 'Why do you have to go on like this when we haven't done anything to you?'

'You should've thought of that before, shouldn't you?'

It was like listening to something on the radio. After all, what could I do? I struggled, in a quiet sort of way, but I have to admit it, I was in no hurry to get free. In fact I thought he'd been bloody idle the way he'd let me get away with the slack like he had done. Obviously no sailor.

'What would you do if I said yes?'

'Yes you'd let us go? I'd say thank you very much.'

'And what would you think?'

'I'd think thank God he's quite a decent chap after all.'

'Thank God, would you?'

'Yes.'

'Look, I don't want you wriggling about, understand? You stay put, do you understand?'

'I'm only trying to get comfortable.'

'Not your job to be comfortable. Get over there a bit.' And would you believe it, he gives me a shove that half rolls me exactly in the direction I want to go. I resisted a bit and that made him push me that much harder into the corner.

'Hullo, are you back?'

He said, 'Go on when I tell you.'

I've never dared to say that to a woman, never. Not even in Amsterdam.

She said, 'You think it's something terrible, don't you?'

'Never mind what I think. Do it, that's all, when I tell you.'

Do you know, I was on his side? At the same time as trying to press my elbows together and turn the rope into a sort of tunnel I could flatten my hands and slip out of. I reckoned I needed five seconds, maybe ten. Which is as long as it takes to run a hundred yards, in other words a lot longer than you think. It's a funny thing, I could imagine it going right and I could imagine it going wrong, and when I imagined it going wrong it never ended with him shooting me, it ended with a sort of laugh and apology from me, a sort of confession that it hadn't come off and naturally he understood and wouldn't take it out on me and could we go back to how we were before? I could see the whole scene working both ways.

'You think you're that ugly, do you?'

'I'm teaching you a lesson,' he said. 'So you may as well get on with it.'

He had his eye on me, I could tell that, but in the nature of things he was more interested in her than in me. That's why he'd gone and got me out of the light. I could see them over my shoulder when I tried. And he'd got her on her knees in front of him. Which, in practical terms, meant that he hadn't got that good a view of me and equally he couldn't get to me that quickly. In addition, he'd inevitably hesitate before shooting, not necessarily because he didn't dare to but because he wouldn't be sure which one of us to go for first, which was what would give me my chance.

'Tell me what you want me to do.'

'Don't start that.'

'In words.'

'You know what I want you to do.'

'In words.'

'You don't seem to understand your position. There are lots more things I can do if I want to.'

'You think you're so ugly, don't you?'

'It means absolutely nothing to me what I do.'

'Do you pity me at all?'

'Why should I?'

'Doing what you want me to do? Do you?'

'Why should I?'

'You think you're punishing me, don't you? By making

me fondle you, as if it was the most terrible thing in the world, to do what you want me to do, as if it was really the most disgusting thing in the world. You think I'll be punished just by touching you. That's what excites you, isn't it? The thought of how disgusting you are and how humiliated I'm going to be.'

'You're just stalling.'

'That it's such an insult.'

'We can be here all night if you like.'

'But what if I loved you—'

'Only I'd advise you—'

'What if I loved you, you poor little sod—'

'I shouldn't insult me—'

'What if I loved you? Could you bear it? That someone should love you and do to you what people do when they love each other, do this terrible thing with love, could you bear that? I love you, I love you.'

'No, you don't—'

'I love you. You're not hurting me, you're not humiliating me because I love you. I love you, even the smell of you I love, I don't mind— you see— you see— you're no good—'

'Shut up. Shut UP.'

'You're no good, you see? Oh it must be awful to be you. I'll tell you what, why don't you take off your clothes, everything, and let me love you like real people love—?'

'I warned you, didn't I?'

'It's too late for warnings. I love you. I accept you. I love you—'

'No you don't. You're just a damned whore and nothing else, nothing else at all. Just a damned whore.'

'Well, what's wrong with that?'

174

'And you don't mean a word you say.'

'Yes I do,' she said. 'I do actually.'

'Lift your skirt up. Lift it up. Go on.'

None of these office buildings have been as well built as they appear, that's something you realize when you're at floor level. The joinery is nothing like up to standard, if Lambert Livingston's office is anything to go by. The skirting board was as much as three-tenths of an inch above the level of the floor in places, although with this thick carpet you couldn't tell unless you looked very carefully. And the lighting fixtures were far from perfect. The masking was by no means straight. There are rough edges everywhere if you look hard. The world seems to be well put together, but any sort of a careful survey reveals flaws everywhere, doesn't it? You get a list of credits as long as your arm on these new buildings—consultant this and consultant that—and they turn out to be rubbish. No one prepared to take responsibility, that's the thing. When you've got one hand free, you've got the other one, although it took me a minute to realize it.

'That's better. And don't try and look at him, because he's not going to help you.'

She said, 'You're just a dirty little runt, a dirty little coward, aren't you? That's all you are.'

'I'm immaterial,' he said.

'I wish you were.'

'What I am, it's not material.'

'Does this really give you pleasure?'

'I'm not interested in pleasure.'

'Much. Not much, you're not.' She sniffed. It was a sad sound. It made me feel very sad, that sniff.

'Now these. Get 'em off. Go on.'

'You poor little bastard.'

'I warned you, didn't I?' He must've hit her across the face. I lay there shaking. It was like being called when you're on your way out of the house. Do you admit you've heard or not? Do you react or don't you? Theoretically I was turned the other way, but that wasn't the point. If I made any sort of commotion he might take a closer look and I didn't want that. I didn't make a sound. I might as well have been on my bus already. Only what was Jeannie thinking?

'If you've broken my glasses—'

'They're all right. I haven't broken anything, I just wanted you to know I wasn't fooling.'

'Oh do what you want,' she said.

'No,' he said, 'that's not enough.'

'No, it wouldn't be, would it?'

The funny thing was, nothing that was happening or had happened seemed in the least bit unlikely any more. Put it this way, it had become a way of life, having this bloke in the room doing what he was doing. People say something's unbelievable but my experience is when a thing's actually happening it doesn't seem in the least unbelievable. It's what's ordinary that becomes unbelievable, not the other way round. I read a paperback in a hotel in Leicester once and this bloke said that there are millions and millions—and even that's an underestimate because it's more like a million to the power of a million—anyway millions and millions of worlds, galaxies, what have you, and this bloke maintained that in that case there's no reason on earth why there shouldn't be places where, for the sake of example, there were people with blue hair or two cocks or what have you, because what's to prevent it? Now there may be a flaw in this argument somewhere along the line, because granite trees or asparagus fish or things like that sound more or less impossible, but it's a thought, isn't it, that everything you can think of may exist or be happening somewhere? I mean, think of all those galaxies where something logically has to be going on? There's no evidence there aren't several more of us, each one of us, somewhere, and every time we come to a crossroads, make a decision, maybe one of us goes one way and one the other. For instance, somewhere, in some galaxy aeons away, I may have not married Lo at all, and maybe I'm a Master Mariner at this point, or a pimp in Singapore. (I wouldn't mind being either.) Maybe we come in all sizes and colours, because assuming the universe contains every possibility, as this bloke maintained, it's more likely than not that everything's happening somewhere.

'Now hold your skirt up, both hands, go on. Right up.'

He was giving himself an airing, I could see that all right. Personally I'm not one to take a great interest in another man. It's not something that interests me in the usual way, looking at other men, frankly it doesn't do anything for me, but there he was and it seemed the most natural thing in the world, although at the same time I was thinking Christ, it's the first time I've ever seen another bloke actually in the countdown position. It was quite a landmark, really, although, as with him looking at the woman in front of him, I daresay it was less of an experience than one expected. It's a long way to China, a bloke I sailed with used to say, but a carrot's still only a carrot. Sid Brennan, I wonder what happened to him.

He was staring at her – tilted the desk lamp to cop a

better view – and I thought, he's trying to get to know her, like a woman'll stare at you when you come home as if she's hoping to read something on your face and if you say anything she thinks you're trying to cover up. Maybe he was shy, maybe he didn't know quite where to put himself (I still think I was right and he'd never actually, you know), maybe he couldn't believe – and that's life, isn't it? – that there wasn't anything more to a woman than that. Sex is a bit of a disappointment, isn't it, after all the brochures frankly, or can be. Without love, I mean. Wouldn't expect me to say that, but it's true in a way, I mean without the preliminaries, isn't it? The terrible thing is, I knew what I had to do, I was all set, but it just needed those last few seconds when I really decided to act and there wasn't any turning back, no time for back-pedalling or soft chat, and I had to nerve myself up to it and I suppose I have to be honest, I sort of wondered what was going to happen, what he'd actually manage to do and, like in a dream when you don't want to wake up before you've seen as much as you want, I didn't like to interrupt the performance until I had to. This wasn't a conscious thing, but I've thought about it since.

I could imagine the smirk on her face, because he obviously couldn't do whatever he wanted to do. He said, 'Lie down on the floor. Do as I say, you'd better.' He'd put on this big voice again, whereas previously he'd been back down to a whisper. I almost fancy she sighed, like a patient when the doctor can't manage something that way and has to try again from the beginning, just when you've keyed yourself up for the pain and you're all set to get it over with. 'Do as I say or you know what'll happen. On your back.'

He was very threatening, which should have been nasty, but in fact, in a way I find it hard to explain, I found it rather touching, as a matter of fact, because it was like he was courting her, the threat was a kind of reassurance, an alibi for her, if you like, so it could be on the record she had no alternative, he may not have thought it that way, but in fact it left her something. Suddenly she was crying out, she was yelling and I was thinking, 'Shut up, you bitch,' and he gave a shout sort of thing and I thought of her saying 'us', how he thought he was frightening us, and what he'd said about us being separate and then I realized that when he gave that shout, which was sort of triumph and pain all in one, us was him and me, not me and her, and that was when I gave him the fire extinguisher right in the face, whoomf.

It was in the corner on this hook, and I'd got onto my side so he couldn't see, even if he'd had eyes to look, that my hands were actually free and I got the appliance off its hook and I've seen these things demonstrated at what seamen call Board of Trade Sports (in any case, there'd been plenty of time to read the instructions again just to be sure) so I knew what to do, it was just a question of the right moment, bang the knob and wallop. I'd postponed it, I admit that, but I was so pleased with my plan, which was, you have to agree, something rather unexpected, that I reckoned I'd get the V.C. anyway so I might as well take my time. Of course there wasn't much distinguishing friend and foe to begin with, I must admit. I twisted myself round as best I could and did what I could to leave Jeannie clear but once I was committed the thing was to make sure I didn't waste anything. He dropped the gun, that was the big thing, and put his hands to his face, because I'd got him right between the eyes and I shouted to Jeannie, 'Get the gun, lie on it, do something,' as if I hated her bloody guts. I couldn't stand up, of course, because of my ankles, so I lurched forward and kept squirting and squirting all this powder. Do you know nine seconds is one hell of a long time? Quite frankly it went on longer than I could conveniently use. I'd long since made my point but it was one of those total discharge models, you couldn't cut it off once you got started. They do that for safety reasons, so you don't leave yourself with only two seconds' worth another time and an oil refinery to put out. The last couple of seconds were sheer murder actually, because the poor little sod was well and truly put out already. He had his hands up, like the last of the Mohicans, but I kept squirting him because I didn't want any regrets afterwards. Jeannie said, 'Shall I shoot him, shall I? I've got the gun.' And I said, 'No, for Christ's sake. You gone mad?'

'I wondered what had happened to you, that's all.'
'Well, I've told you what happened, haven't I?'
'I suppose so.'
'I had a meeting, didn't I?'

I said, 'Go on, scoot.'
He just stood there. It was as if he still didn't realize that he hadn't got the gun any more, that he hadn't got the slightest hold over us, that he was very lucky to be in one piece. He actually looked resentful. He looked hurt, as if he couldn't believe we didn't want him any more. He was really pained.
'Scoot, I said.'

He was wiping this powder off his clothes and out of his ears. You could see him thinking about the cleaners. His eyes were watering. He looked terrible and he couldn't make himself go.

'You'd better get going.'

He thought I was a right bully, you could see it in his face. I suppose the gun had set him back a few bob. He kept staring at it, hanging down in my hand. Or maybe he'd borrowed it and was wondering what he was going to say to the bloke. Do you know what I did? You may not believe this – I bunged him a couple of quid, stuffed it in his pocket. He still wouldn't go, though.

'You're lucky we haven't called the police.'

'Am I?' he said. He had her there. This crafty, weepy little smile came over his face. And then he found some more muck under his collar and flicked it on the floor in front of him.

'Look,' I said, 'I'll give you five. I'll start counting and you've got five to be on your way.'

He was almost grateful. I'd come up with a reasonable formula. He stayed till three and then he was gone. One second he was there, the next the doorway was empty. He did have a moped too, because I heard him starting the bloody thing. Unmistakable. I never saw if he had a crash helmet though because Jeannie had started sniffing, long, quavery sniffs, horrible sound.

'God,' she said, 'God –'

I could've killed her, that's the truth. I turned and I smiled at her and all she could do was sniff. No congratulations, nothing. I gave her my cheeky how-about-that-then look and she sniffed and you know what she was doing? She was tidying up. She was bloody well tidying up. I said, 'What're you doing for Christ's sake?' and she said, 'Tidying up. We've got our work cut out after what you've done.' 'Work? Fuck work.' 'How are you going to explain this?' she said. 'Explain it? Are you potty? This is nothing to do with us. We're not having anything to do with this.' And I gave her my look again, only I might as well have been muck. I went up to her and I was thinking, 'kiss me,' I was thinking, 'kiss me, you bitch, go on, go on, what're you waiting for?' and all she was doing was she was putting her pants on and at the same time trying to scoop the powder off the green leather on Lambert Livingston's desk. 'Remember me? Charlie Hanson.' 'The next best thing to handsome,' she said. I stuck the gun in her ribs and I grinned and said, 'Give us a kiss then, girl.' She brushed me off like a cobweb. I put my arm round her. I couldn't believe it, she was fighting me, she was actually fighting me. 'Get off me.' I put the gun on the desk and I said, 'What's the idea?' and I grabbed her. I pushed her down on the ground in the snow and I thought, 'By Christ, you're not getting away with it again,' and she was fighting, she was fighting, I honestly think she was fighting me harder than she had old Murg and I thought fuck you, by Christ I did. I could have killed her. I thought, right, you hate me and I'll hate you and we'll see how you like it. Damned lucky I'm not wringing your bloody neck. Not much love left, you might say. And you'd be right. You know what she did afterwards? She just pushed me off and went and got the Hoover out of the cupboard in the vestibule. I picked up the gun and I brushed myself off and I went out and I banged the door as hard as I could. Cow.

182

Nowadays Lo says to me sometimes, 'You know Charlie, I really think we're happier now than we've ever been, don't you, in some ways?' 'In some ways, yes.' 'I think we are,' she says and she gives me this lovely smile and there's a sort of look in her eye that I have to respond to, but it makes me a little hot somewhere, to tell you the truth. The trouble with women is, give them a chance and they think they own you. Never mind, I've still got the gun.